Katy Keene

Restless Hearts

Katy Keene

Restless Hearts

An original prequel novel by
STEPHANIE KATE STROHM

SCHOLASTIC INC.

Copyright © 2020 by Archie Comic Publications, Inc.

All rights reserved. Published by Scholastic Inc., *Publishers since 1920.* SCHOLASTIC and associated logos are trademarks and/or registered trademarks of Scholastic Inc.

The publisher does not have any control over and does not assume any responsibility for author or third-party websites or their content.

No part of this publication may be reproduced, stored in a retrieval system, or transmitted in any form or by any means, electronic, mechanical, photocopying, recording, or otherwise, without written permission of the publisher. For information regarding permission, write to Scholastic Inc., Attention: Permissions Department, 557 Broadway, New York, NY 10012.

This book is a work of fiction. Names, characters, places, and incidents are either the product of the author's imagination or are used fictitiously, and any resemblance to actual persons, living or dead, business establishments, events, or locales is entirely coincidental.

ISBN 978-1-338-67631-0

1 2020

Printed in the U.S.A.   23

First printing 2020

Book design by Heather Daugherty

Photo © Shutterstock.com

FOR MY DAD. SEE, I REALLY *DID* NEED
YOU TO BUY ME THE ENTIRE ARCHIE
AMERICANA SERIES.
–S.K.S.

CHAPTER ONE
Katy

I HAVE *ALWAYS* LOVED FALL.

It's the perfect season, especially in New York: the colors, the brisk weather, all the fashion-layering opportunities. Plus, there's the September issue of *Vogue*, New York Fashion Week, beautiful new displays in all the department store windows . . . But I've loved fall since before I could even pronounce "Anna Wintour." It's probably because of back-to-school shopping.

Every year, my mom took me uptown to Lacy's so we could browse the sale racks. But more often than not, we'd just look at the glamorous window displays for inspiration, then go home so Mom could create her own versions of the outfits we couldn't quite afford, teaching me how to sew at her side. Bergdorf and Bloomingdale's and Barneys may have their devoted followers, but none of those stores even come close to Lacy's. Every time I walk through her famous double doors with the stained-glass panels, designed by Louis Comfort Tiffany himself, I get the sense that nothing bad can happen to you there.

Lacy's is high-end enough to be aspirational, but timeless enough to be accessible. If Lacy's was a person, she would be a woman in a perfectly tailored suit. Something classic, that would never go out of style.

Lacy's is an American icon.

But despite all this, my favorite part will always be the windows. Mom and I came every year to see the displays change with the seasons, back when I was small enough to be strapped to her chest in a baby carrier. But this was the first fall I was at Lacy's on my own.

No Mom.

I clutched my coffee a little tighter, blinking as I focused on the window display. Mom wouldn't want me to cry at Lacy's. It would be all wrong, like crying at Disney World.

The mannequins in the window all had silk scarves trailing from their necks, almost like Amelia Earhart. Little-known fact: Amelia Earhart actually designed a fashion line in the 1930s, and they carried it exclusively at Lacy's. I stepped closer to admire a pair of high-waisted tweed pants, a pair of oxford heels peeping out from under the hems. Absolutely the kind of thing a daring aviatrix might sport. Amelia would definitely approve.

"Happy fall, Katy Keene."

I turned, and there was my boyfriend, KO Kelly,

standing in the middle of the busy sidewalk, holding a donut. There's something about a six-foot-one heavyweight boxer holding a confection covered in pink frosting and rainbow sprinkles that's just too perfect for words. He folded me into his arms, careful to keep the frosting from rubbing against the red Peter Pan collar of my wool coat, resting his chin on top of my head. There's no safer place than wrapped in KO's arms.

Well, except maybe Lacy's.

"I know I'm not your mom, Katy, but I didn't want you to be on your own for the unveiling of the Lacy's windows."

So sweet. I rose up on my tiptoes to kiss him, and I melted a little, just like I always did.

"Is that donut for me?" I asked.

"Oh yeah." KO blushed. "I, uh, ate mine on the walk from the subway. But here." He handed over the donut, and I bit in, relishing the sweet sugar rush. Delicious. "Nothing but Plunkin' Donuts' finest for my girl."

"So," I asked in between mouthfuls, "what do you think?"

I gestured to the window in front of me, and KO turned to contemplate it fully.

"This is really . . ." His brow furrowed as he looked in the window like he was hoping an answer might fly out of the caramel-colored beret on the mannequin closest to us. "Um . . . pants? Those are some nice pants?"

"Oh, yes, I agree," I said seriously. "Very pants."

"I'm sorry; my fashion expertise is limited to boxing gear!" He picked me up and spun me around as we laughed, sprinkles scattering onto the sidewalk.

Being here, with KO, was the first time since Mom died that I felt like I could remember her without the beep of machines, the faded fabric of her hospital gown, and the smell of the terrible food. I remembered her here, at Lacy's, sketching what she saw in the window on a crumpled napkin or the back of a receipt.

"Well? Shall we?" KO offered me his arm.

"Shall we what? Go in?" I raised an eyebrow skeptically. "Unfortunately, I'm not exactly in the market for a new fall wardrobe right now. Number one priority is figuring out how I'm going to pay the rent."

I was still in the apartment on the Lower East Side that I'd grown up in, but I had a feeling that wouldn't last for much longer. I was doing my best to find a job, but at the moment, I could barely scrape together what I owed each month. And although the landlord had been really understanding ever since Mom got sick, from our last couple of conversations, I was getting the sense that Mr. Discenza was thinking of selling the building. He could probably make a lot more money selling it to some developer than he was currently collecting in rent, now that the neighborhood was getting increasingly trendy, even as far east as we were. A spin studio had opened up on our block last week, which meant it was really the beginning of the end. It was no longer the Delancey Street of my childhood.

"You're taking 'window-shopping' a bit too literally." Gently, KO tugged me toward the revolving doors, and we squeezed in together, KO's bulk taking up most of the space. "You're allowed to look at more than just the displays."

As we emerged onto the marble-tiled floor, the atrium expansive above us, I breathed in the scent of hundreds of perfumes commingling.

"Ambition by Rex London?" a spritzer asked. I paused, admiring how chic her high-necked black blouse was, with the small, surprising floral detail at the collar that kept it from being too staid.

KO sneezed in response.

"No, thank you." I smiled, steering my boyfriend to the less-scented air of the clothing departments. He was still sneezing as we stepped onto the escalator, his normally clear blue eyes red.

I gripped KO's arm excitedly, wondering what they'd have upstairs. Obviously, I was excited to see the new designs, but it wasn't just about a new pair of suede boots. It was about what those boots *represented*. The changing of seasons. Saying good-bye to the old to bring in the new.

A fresh start.

And this year, I really needed a fresh start.

"You know what I decided?" I said as we rode up to women's wear, the sounds of the perfume hall disappearing behind us.

"What's that?"

"I've decided this is going to be the best fall ever."

My final year of high school had been swallowed up by the pain of slowly losing Mom, knowing there was nothing I could do. I barely even remembered last fall. But this was a new season, full of nothing but possibility, and I was going to do everything I could to make the most of it.

"The best fall ever, huh?" KO grinned, hopping off the escalator behind me. "I don't know about that. What about the fall of freshman year, when I saw the prettiest girl I'd ever seen, walking down Second Avenue in a bright red coat?"

"Better than that." I grinned, too, remembering how I'd almost walked into a trash can because I'd been so distracted by the cute boy in the Western Queens Boxing Gym jacket.

"What about the fall of sophomore year, when I finally got the courage to ask her out?"

"Even better than that." I flung my arms around his neck and kissed him, right there in the middle of women's wear. "It's going to be perfect. We'll watch the leaves change color in Central Park and sip hot cider, and we can take the train to that pick-your-own apple orchard on Long Island . . ."

"And we'll eat, sleep, and breathe pumpkin spice," KO finished for me, suppressing a laugh.

"What are *your* plans for the most fabulous fall ever?" I punched him on the arm jokingly. I doubt he even felt it.

"Probably spending most of it inside. At the boxing

gym." KO shrugged sheepishly. "Now that I've graduated, I can really get serious about my career. The journey to Madison Square Garden starts now, baby." I laughed as he shadowboxed the mannequin in front of us, throwing a neat cross toward her cashmere-clad torso. "Actually . . ." KO pulled his phone out of his pocket, checking the time. "I'm meeting Jinx to train in just a couple hours."

"Jinx?" I asked. I knew all of KO's sparring partners—sometimes we'd go out to the Starlite Diner together after a match, either celebrating their victories or drowning our sorrows in the best milk shakes in Queens—and I'd definitely never heard the name Jinx before.

"Newest boxer at the gym. Absolutely incredible." KO's eyes lit up the way mine did when the silk charmeuse was on sale at Mood Fabrics. "I've had to seriously step up my game. It's been awesome."

Well, whoever this Jinx was, he must really be something. Usually the only thing that made KO gush like this was Starlite's chili cheese fries on days that he didn't have a weigh-in.

"Well, thanks to Jinx for sparing you, and thank *you* for coming all the way in from Queens before heading right back out there again." I squeezed his hand, and he kept hold of it, his fingers threading through mine.

"Forget it. A little interborough travel is nothing. I would cross oceans for you, Katy Keene."

His tone was joking, but I knew he meant it, cheesy as it was. He'd done something much harder than cross an ocean for me. He'd been by my side, every step of the way, while Mom was sick. He'd held my hand in the hospital waiting room. He'd brought dinner on all those nights when I'd forgotten to eat. And when Mom was gone, he'd refused to let me be alone; he brought me home to his family on Long Island, where I could disappear for a bit into the warmth and noise and love of the Kelly family.

If it hadn't been for KO, I don't know what would have happened to me.

"I don't want to disrespect your beloved Lacy's, Katy, but the clothes you make are way better than ninety percent of the stuff I've seen on the racks today. They should be selling *your* designs." KO tugged on the sleeve of a sweater near us, frowning distastefully. "What even is this?"

I frowned at the sweater right along with him. One sleeve was covered in sequins. The other was entirely mesh. And there was a saguaro cactus appliquéd on the front that appeared to be bleeding.

Well, not all fashion risks paid off.

"You're very sweet, KO, but I'm not a real designer." I made almost all of my own clothes, and my ultimate dream was to have my own fashion line someday, but that still felt like such a long way off. The idea of Lacy's selling my clothes seemed about as likely as one of my dresses being modeled on the moon. "Not yet, anyway. Someday, I hope, but—"

My phone vibrated in my purse. I jumped, scrambling to open the tricky vintage clasp, thinking it might be the hospital, before remembering that they had no reason to call me anymore. Shoulders slumping, I realized this was only the first of many times I'd forget that Mom was gone.

"Are you going to get that?" KO asked.

"Yeah; I'm sure it's nothing." I pulled the vibrating phone out, then stared at the screen in confusion. "Huh."

"Who is it?"

"It's Veronica," I said. "Veronica Lodge."

I hadn't heard from Veronica in a while. We'd had that wonderful shopping day together when she came in for her Barnard interview, and she'd sent me a very tasteful fruit basket when Mom died, but we didn't usually talk on the phone. We were more the make-plans-over-text types, and then once we were together, in person, it was like no time had passed at all.

Veronica Lodge. I stared at the phone. *What could she possibly have to talk to me about?*

Well, there was only one way to find out.

I pressed "accept" and lifted the phone to my ear.

CHAPTER TWO
Jorge

HELLO DARKNESS, MY OLD FRIEND . . .

Light streamed in through the kitchen windows—as long as Mr. Ramos next door kept using his lot to rent out monthly parking spaces, we'd always have the sunniest apartment in Washington Heights—but I couldn't help humming a little Simon and Garfunkel to myself. The soundtrack to today's breakfast, like it had been for every breakfast since I moved back home, was nothing but the sound of silence.

I should have just grabbed an egg-and-cheese from our bodega downstairs on my way to Broadway Dance Center, but Ma had been making such a big deal about eating together, as a *family*.

Which was ironic, because sitting in silence completely ignoring one another was not how the Lopez family usually operated. Back when all my brothers were at home, it was a riot of noise. With Joaquin pushing Ma out of the kitchen so he could cook some cut of meat nobody had ever heard of, Hugo icing his shoulder, Alejandro buried in his econ books, and Miguel and Mateo teasing each other, it was so loud you couldn't hear yourself think.

I wished I couldn't hear myself think.

Instead, all I heard was the scrape of a knife as Dad spread butter across a slice of wheat toast. My spoon clinked against the cereal bowl. The pages fluttered in Ma's magazine as she finished one article and moved on to the next one.

So much left unsaid. All of us afraid to say it.

Why did they even ask me to come home if they are just going to keep pretending I don't exist?

"Well, I should probably get going." Dad cleared his throat and stood up abruptly, a half-eaten piece of toast still in one hand. "We may be restructuring the plowing pattern in the district. Gotta get that done before the first snowfall."

"Wow, another thrilling day in the life of a city councilman," I muttered. "Get out there and feel the fantasy, Dad."

He kissed Ma on the cheek, waved vaguely in my direction without bothering to look at me, and left, munching on his toast.

"He's trying, m'hijo," Ma said softly once we heard the door shut behind him.

"Trying *what*? Trying to fill his mustache with crumbs? Dad is serving some Latino Tom Selleck realness, if

Tom Selleck tried to eat his way out of an IHOP, mustache-first."

Mom laughed softly, and just said, "We're *all* trying."

If *this* was what trying looked like, the Lopezes would have to learn to try a lot harder. It had been three years since I'd come home, and it still felt like nothing had changed. How had we been doing this for so long? I wanted things to change, but it wasn't on me to make some kind of grand filial gesture and start playing happy family again. *They* were the ones who kicked *me* out. At only fourteen! If Katy and her mom hadn't taken me in, who knows what would have happened to me. Most gay kids who are forced to leave home end up on the streets; they aren't nearly so lucky.

And now Katy's mom was gone. Losing the mother figure who had *always* accepted me for who I was just made my situation at home feel even more messed up. I missed her with an ache that would sometimes sneak up on me and snatch my breath away. My mom may have been right here, but it felt like we'd never been farther apart.

Ma stood up and patted me on the shoulder. She placed her magazine in front of me, very deliberately, then left, probably to go downstairs and rearrange stock, since she never approved of anybody else's shelving. Ma treated the bodega like her own personal HGTV show, except instead of slapping shiplap on everything that wasn't nailed down, she was on an endless quest for the optimal place-ment of Chex Mix and Hot Fries. I turned her magazine toward me. It was an old issue of *People*—the cover story was about some *Matchelorette* star I barely remembered and her newfound "Baby Joy!"; the infant wrinkly and red, half of her head obscured by an obscenely large bow.

If Ma thought this was the kind of thing I'd be interested in, she understood me even less than I'd thought. Even with my summer of nothing, I had better things to do than watch a bunch of walking hair extensions fight over some bland white guy with veneers. Plus, it took a very special head shape to pull off a headpiece that dramatic, and this poor baby had not been blessed in that department.

Rolling my eyes, I grabbed my empty cereal bowl and the magazine, dropping the bowl in the sink and tossing the magazine back onto the kitchen counter next to the stack of unopened mail. The magazine slid along the counter, and something dropped out of it, landing on the floor with a smack.

"Great." I sank down onto my knees with a slight creak—if I was feeling this stiff already, dance class was going to be *brutal*—and picked it up, expecting an insert advertisement for butt-lifting leggings or cellulite-slimming sneakers or maybe giant, face-obscuring baby bows. Instead, it was an issue of *Backstage*, folded open to a page of casting calls.

Huh. *Backstage* wasn't something we carried at the bodega. I had an online membership where I could search all the latest audition notices, but I'd let it lapse. My plan had been to spend the summer auditioning for stuff, now that I was finally done with high school and could really devote myself to making it on Broadway, but summer had turned out to be kind of a dead season. At first, I'd tried to look for a show that would make me eligible for Equity, the actors' union, so I could actually work on Broadway, but there wasn't anything. Turned out, there wasn't even any non-Equity work, either. All those actors were out of the city, doing regional summer stock, and even if I miraculously could have gotten an audition for a Broadway show that didn't require an Equity card (which I didn't have), or an agent (which I also didn't have), or an appointment (almost impossible to get without the first two things), nothing was casting. It had been so easy to settle into a routine of silent meals, dance classes, shifts at the bodega, and hiding in my room, losing myself in endless marathons of *RuPaul's Drag Race*.

I'd love to see what those queens could do with some giant baby bows.

But now that it was fall, *something* must have been casting, since one of the audition notices in *Backstage* was circled in black Sharpie. Obviously, Ma had left it here for me to find. I'd prefer it if she talked to me instead of communicating through casting calls hidden inside *People* magazine, but if I'd learned anything over the last couple of years, it was that the Lopezes weren't as good at talking as they thought they were.

At first glance, I thought the casting call might have been a joke. Ethan Fox was directing a revival of *Hello,*

Dolly! Ethan Fox? That didn't make any sense. Ethan Fox was a darling of the daring off-Broadway scene. His last show had been a new work in an abandoned button factory on the Lower East Side in which all the actors wore raw meat that literally decayed on their bodies over the run of the show. Only a genius like Ethan Fox could bring back the meat dress from its 2010-Gaga-at-the-VMAs heyday and make it revelatory instead of played out. Ben Brantley at the *New York Times* had said something funny about the show that I couldn't quite remember, about how if you could stand the smell, it was stunning. Ethan Fox wouldn't touch a musical with a ten-foot pole. And certainly not one as old-school as *Hello, Dolly!*

And yet . . . there it was, in black-and-white in *Backstage*: Ethan Fox was holding open call auditions for a Broadway revival of *Hello, Dolly!* I gripped the magazine tighter, my pulse speeding up against my will.

Open call?

An open call, where anyone could show up and be seen, was a *huge* opportunity for a non-Equity Broadway hopeful like me. And an unusual one. I couldn't remember there being an open call for a Broadway show since the *Hair* revival in '09. I'd been way too young to audition then—especially for a show that required full-frontal nudity—but Ma and I had watched a story about it on the news. Willie Geist had interviewed actors standing in a line that wound around the block, all of them waiting for their chance to be seen.

Could this be *my* chance?

I scanned the rest of the casting notice, hoping there might be a principal role I'd be a good fit for. Obviously, even being in the chorus would be amazing—I'd be fast-tracked into Equity, plus I'd be a real working actor, on *Broadway*—but a speaking role would be even more amazing.

There. Down at the bottom of the casting notice. They were looking for a strong dancer, male, any ethnicity, ages 18 to 21, to play Barnaby Tucker.

It only takes a moment.

That was the love song in *Hello, Dolly!* I hummed a couple of bars. In musicals, it only took a moment to fall in love, which was kind of ridiculous, but it was possible for everything to change in a moment in real life, too.

This could be my moment.

I ripped the page out of *Backstage* and folded it neatly into quarters, then stuck it in the pocket of my sweatpants.

I had no idea what an Ethan Fox production of *Hello, Dolly!* could possibly look like.

But I knew I was going to find out.

CHAPTER THREE
Pepper

"BRITISH INVASION!"

by Amelie Stafford for *CelebutanteTalk*,
a subsidiary of Cabot Media

Hold on to your knickers, fellow Yanks, because things are about to get SPICY in the city that never sleeps! That's right, Pepper Smith herself is reportedly heading back to New York City, allegedly leaving one heartbroken royal rascal behind her in England.

Love her or hate her, we know you know her, but in case you've spent the last couple years on Mars, let's recap: Daddy Smith is based in Hong Kong, where he does something too complicated and too lucrative for us mere mortals to understand, but the multilingual baby Pepper grew up all over the world, eventually acquiring that swoony accent while being educated at the finest schools in London.

Those buttoned-up Brits couldn't get enough of the plucky Pepper. Whether she was putting the love in "forty-love" with a certain gorgeous tennis champ at Wimbledon, exhibiting her original work at the Tate Modern to astounding critical acclaim, or wearing nothing but a truly giant hat to Ladies' Day at Ascot, it was smashing success after smashing success across the pond. Even one well-known, particularly shiny-haired duchess was overheard remarking that she was "obsessed" with everything Pepper! And, TBH, who wouldn't be?

With rumors swirling about a certain royal affair (rumors we wouldn't dare repeat—unlike those nasty British tabloids, we here at *CelebutanteTalk* understand a little something called journalistic integrity!), Pepper is stateside for the foreseeable future, and we lucky New Yorkers couldn't be happier! Pepper has been keeping uncharacteristically mum about her next steps (perhaps the influence of those stiff-upper-lipped Brits?), but knowing the inimitable Miss Smith, she's sure to have something unbelievable up her (couture) sleeve!

CHAPTER FOUR
Josie

I WAS BARELY OUT OF high school, and I'd already made it on Broadway.

Well, fine, it was Broadway Street in Michigan, but the Detroit Opera House was nothing to sneeze at. I stood in the wings, peeking out at the rows of red velvet seats slowly filling with patrons, the ornate golden balconies, and the gorgeous domed ceiling.

"It's one of my favorite venues in the country." Dad appeared behind me, looking out over my shoulder. "I always make sure every tour I do books a show in Detroit."

Since I left Riverdale to go on the road with Dad, we'd been getting along pretty well—no, really well, actually. Maybe the best we'd ever gotten along.

"Remember this moment," Dad continued, squeezing my shoulder. "Really remember it. How it feels, how it looks, how it smells, everything. Three thousand seats, full of people who are here to see *you*."

"They're here to see *you*, Dad." I couldn't resist rolling my eyes a little. My name wasn't even on the ticket.

"Sure, maybe that's why they *came*. But they'll leave remembering your name."

I glowed with pride. When he wasn't on my case about messing with the tempo—I swear, that man had an inner metronome you could set your watch by—Dad had been surprisingly complimentary about my singing. After years of desperately seeking his approval and constantly falling short, it was a nice change of pace.

"I'll certainly give them something to remember." I hummed softly, vocalizing the descant in our opening number. Impostor syndrome has never been one of my issues, and I knew I'd never sounded better. This was what I was meant to do: sing, professionally, night after night.

And I loved every minute of it.

"Remember this, Josie," Dad said again, giving my shoulder one final squeeze. "Because it won't always be like this. You'll need to remember all the glamour and gold when we're singing in the back of a TGI Thursday's on National Baby Back Rib Day."

"Very funny, Dad."

"And watch the tempo on the bridge in the first number!" He walked farther backstage to talk to one of the sound guys.

"Dad. Um, Dad?" Forget the tempo on the bridge. He

couldn't be serious . . . right? "Are we really playing a TGI Thursday's?"

"Five minutes until places." A stage manager crossed by, adjusting her headset and glancing at a clipboard. It was strange to be in a different place with a different crew every night. True, the "crew" at La Bonne Nuit had mostly just been Reggie with a spotlight, but there was something so weird about doing the same show night after night, where the set list was mostly the same, but everything around us changed.

I rolled my shoulders back, hearing them crack. The Comfort Motel we'd stayed in last night hadn't exactly lived up to its name, with its hard-as-a-rock mattress and flat pillows, and my body was feeling it tonight. Luckily, the choreography in Dad's show was mostly of the sing-and-sway variety, not quite like the moves I used to bust out with the Pussycats.

The Pussycats. Thinking about them always gave me a little pause. I was pretty sure I was meant to be a solo artist, but back when things were good, making music with Val and Melody had been some of the best times of my life.

Problem was, those good times had kept getting fewer and farther between. Our end had been inevitable.

So why did I find myself missing them at the oddest of times? I should have been focusing on the show we were about to do, for *three thousand* people, not miles away and years ago, in a dingy music room in a high school with an underfunded arts department.

We had a different opening act in every city we played, one that had been coordinated either by the venue, or more often by Pauly, Dad's tour manager. I watched from backstage as our Detroit opener walked out, a cute Black guy a couple years older than me in a slim velvet suit. He took a seat at the piano, angling the microphone toward his face. Total young John Legend vibes.

"Ooh, another jazz pianist." Dad was back at my shoulder as our opening act played a few chords, his fingers stretching gracefully across the keys. "Shoulda told the venue not to book my competition."

"Don't worry, Dad. There's nobody quite like Myles McCoy."

I knew Dad certainly thought so. But he had the talent to back up his arrogance, and in show business, that was all that mattered. This other guy was good, though. His voice had a warm, rich quality that made me think of a pat of butter melting on a stack of the Chock'lit Shoppe's finest chocolate chip pancakes. I'd had pancakes in diners on the road, but so far, nobody could make a pancake quite like Pop Tate.

"I think I might go out tonight," I said suddenly, wondering what else Detroit might have to offer. If our opener was this good, who knew what other talent was out there. Actually, I should probably ask this guy where to go. Someone who pulled off a velvet suit that well must have some kind of idea of what was happening around town. I had a hard time imagining he was heading home to sit on the couch and watch the *Matchelorette* while eating cheese puffs after the show.

"Out?" Dad pushed up the brim of his signature fedora, scratching at his forehead.

"Yeah, Dad, out. See something besides a Comfort Motel vending machine. We're in Motor City! The birthplace of Motown. Think of all the incredible voices who started here. The Supremes, the Marvelettes, Mary Wells—"

"Yes, Josie, I'm familiar. No need to read the Motown Museum brochure to me."

"I don't want to go to the museum. I mean, I do, maybe tomorrow," I amended. "But tonight I'd like to hear some live music. See who might be the *next* Mary Wells."

"I don't think that's such a good idea." Dad shook his head slowly, and my heart sank. True, I was eighteen—technically an adult—but this was his show and his rules. I'd learned quickly that out on the road, it was Myles McCoy's world, and everyone else was just living in it. "Wandering around in a city you don't know late at night? That sounds like you're just asking for trouble."

"Dad. I grew up in *Riverdale*." I couldn't resist rolling my eyes. "Suburbia's murder capital. The cutest lil haven of serial killers, organ-snatching cults, and drug-dealing gangs you ever did see. The place where trouble finds you, whether or not you're asking for it." Dad grunted in response. "You were with me when Pop's got shot up. You've seen it for yourself! I think I can handle Detroit."

"Be that as it may . . ." The opener finished and stood up, executing a neat bow as the audience applauded appreciatively. Man, the noise of three thousand people clapping sounded *good*. "Even if you don't run into any hoodlums wearing gremlin masks—"

"Gargoyles," I interrupted him. "And I think that was just a Riverdale thing. Plus, it was two years ago."

"I don't think it's a good idea," Dad concluded. "Now that you're a professional, you have to act like one. Taking care of yourself is your number one priority, and sometimes that means missing out on the fun stuff. Go to sleep early. Save your voice. Rest. So *you* can be the next Mary Wells."

"Can we maybe go to the Motown Museum tomorrow morning, at least?" I asked as the emcee came back out onstage to introduce Dad.

"No time." Dad rolled his shoulders back, his charming stage persona smile already in place. "We've gotta hit the road early to get to Toledo in time to prep for tomorrow's gig. The crew there is notoriously finicky about sound check."

"And here he is, the man you've been waiting for . . . Mister Myles McCoy!"

The emcee flung his arm toward the wing we were waiting in, and Dad walked out, his smile wide, waving at the crowd who greeted him with a roar. I'll say this for the jazz fans in Detroit: They weren't quiet.

Dad sat down at the piano, flipping the back of his

jacket neatly behind him on the bench. A couple people in the crowd whooped as he played a few chords, then a couple arpeggios. I could practically feel the contented sigh in the theater as the notes resolved themselves into the opening of Duke Ellington's "In a Sentimental Mood." Dad frequently started the show alone at the piano, playing this song. It was one of his favorites.

Listening to him play, I had a rare memory of him and my mom at home together, happy, when I was really little. I remembered Dad playing this song, Mom resting a hand on his shoulder, until she pulled him up off the piano so they could dance, Dad humming the melody in his rich baritone as they swayed back and forth.

I wondered how Mom was doing. At first it had been kind of nice to get a break from Sierra McCoy and her never-ending expectations of excellence, but I missed her, too. At least I could be sure that Mr. Keller was taking good care of her. And she'd probably enjoyed bossing Kevin around, before he left for college.

Kevin . . . he'd been so busy with school, and I'd been so busy with touring, we'd barely talked. I had no idea what he was up to. I made a mental note to text my favorite stepbrother after the show. I hadn't really talked to anyone from Riverdale since I left on tour. My world had gotten so much bigger—in the sense that I was in a different city every night, and they were all new to me—but in some ways, it had also gotten so much smaller. It had shrunk to the stage and the motels and the van that took us between the two, and sometimes, it was hard to remember that the world back home kept right on spinning without me.

The audience erupted into applause. Once it died down, Dad launched into some of his onstage patter. For someone who could be so rigid and demanding, I was always surprised by how relaxed and easygoing he seemed onstage, like he was just having a casual chat with three thousand of his closest friends. But then again, he'd always been at his best behind a microphone.

I knew how that felt.

"Sometimes," Dad said, "a special song needs a special voice."

That was my cue. I walked out to the microphone stage left of Dad, the height adjusted perfectly by a stagehand. I wrapped my hands around the microphone and felt a faint hum of electricity, of possibility, of that perfect moment right before I started singing when anything could happen. I could feel the whole audience waiting with me, expectantly, and I knew I wouldn't let them down.

There was a lot of stuff in my life I wasn't sure about. But this? Me and the microphone? This, I *got*.

"Here she is, ladies and gentlemen—my daughter, Miss Josie McCoy!"

Before we left, I hadn't been sure if Dad was going to tell people I was his daughter. I'd been surprised that he ended up making such a big deal out of it in the show. The cynical part of me wondered if it was because it played well with the middle-aged women who comprised the majority of his audience—they all thought it was too cute for words, as they loved to tell me and Dad when they hung around the stage door after our shows, asking Dad for selfies and autographs on their programs—but I hoped it was at least partly because he was proud of me and my talent, too.

Well, if he wasn't proud, exactly, he was at least giving me fewer notes than when we started the tour, and that was something, too.

Dad stopped with the chatter, and looked over at me, his eyebrows raised slightly. I nodded. I was ready.

I took a deep breath, closed my eyes, and sang, Gershwin's words and the notes flowing out of me like magic. After singing the first verse of "Someone to Watch Over Me" a cappella, Dad joined in, the piano instrumentation lush and full. I couldn't see the audience as they sat in the dark, but I could feel them, transported along by the music just like I was. I sang like I'd heard Ella sing it on my dad's old records, but I sang it like me, too.

I didn't need someone to watch over me. Life in Riverdale had taken care of that. No, I was perfectly fine on my own, no shepherd needed.

All I needed was music.

CHAPTER FIVE
Katy

"VERONICA?" I ASKED, ANSWERING THE PHONE.

"Katy!" Something whirred in the background of the call; something I couldn't quite place. Knowing Veronica, it was equally likely to be a Gulfstream jet or a blender. "How is the most gorgeous girl in Manhattan?"

"If I see her, I'll ask." I caught sight of my reflection in one of the million Lacy's mirrors. There were dark circles under my eyes that concealer couldn't quite cover up, and I was too thin, my coat hanging off me. The unfamiliar angles in my face that made me look like a stranger. All those nights of forgetting to eat or being too emotionally exhausted to make dinner had taken a toll. Hopefully, with a few more trips to Plunkin' Donuts, I'd look like myself again soon.

"You're too modest. But seriously, Katy, I was so sorry to hear about your mom." There was a catch in Veronica's voice, and I found myself blinking back tears, too. "What an absolute icon. There are so few women who have true style, and she had it in spades. I'll never forget the dress she made for my quinceañera."

I smiled. I wouldn't, either. Manhattan high society had been shocked when *the* Veronica Lodge had chosen to eschew an established designer label for the most important dress of her life and had gone instead with some nobody who had a tiny little shop specializing in alterations on the Lower East Side. Well, they'd been shocked until they saw the dress—it was stunning.

"Thanks, V." I smiled. "She always said you had a great eye."

"Coming from the Audrey Hepburn of Delancey Street? Now, that's a real compliment." Mom would have *loved* that comparison. *Funny Face* had been one of our favorite movies to watch together. "How are *you* coping, Katy? I hope you've still got that extremely handsome set of broad shoulders to cry on."

"Of course." KO seemed to be on a mission to find the ugliest sweaters in Lacy's history. He marched over now, holding a new one trimmed with gold fringe and covered in rainbow pom-poms. Laughing, I waved him away. "KO's been amazing."

"Good. You deserve nothing less. Now, I've got a bit of news that I hope might help *you* feel a little bit more amazing. If I've learned anything since I turned my talents toward all matters entrepreneurial, it's that keeping busy can be the best thing for a broken heart."

Busy. Busy would be good. Busy with a paycheck would be even better. When KO headed back out to the boxing gym in Queens, I resolved to head home and really dedicate myself to finding a job.

"What's the news?" I asked.

"Hold on to your chapeau," Veronica said. "Lacy's is hosting a fashion show."

"A fashion show? Here?! I didn't think they did those anymore!"

Back in the early and mid-twentieth century, Lacy's had two fashion shows every year so designers could show off their fall and spring lines to the Manhattan elite, but they had become extinct with the rise of fast fashion in the '80s. An in-store fashion show was so charmingly old-school, and such an awesome way to really bring the designer to the consumer.

"Yes, isn't it just too retro-chic for words?!" I could tell Veronica was as excited as I was. "But I haven't even told you the best part yet. Or, best *parts*, I should say. You know Rex London?"

"Of course." Who *didn't*? Even if you weren't part of the fashion world, everyone knew Rex London. He'd become famous as a contestant on *Project Catwalk*, the reality TV fashion design competition show, which had then led to his own show, *What We Wear Now with Rex London*. Plus, he now designed red carpet gowns for celebrities, had his own couture line, and sold less expensive ready-to-wear versions of those couture outfits, and he even had his own fragrance. Last I heard he was releasing a cookbook. Rex London was *everywhere*.

"Well, believe it or not, sweet little Rex used to be the best personal shopper at Lacy's, and *I* was his number one client."

"Really?!" I couldn't believe Veronica knew Rex London! Well, I could—it was Veronica—but even for V, that was really something. Wow. Rex London, a personal shopper at *Lacy's*! What a way to get started in the fashion industry. *That must have been a dream job.*

"Yes, really! Of course I haven't seen him in ages, but we're still friendly. It's always *so* important to have someone you can text for a completely honest opinion on your outfit."

"Mmm-hmmm." I didn't want to be rude, but I was dying for Veronica to get to the point about what Rex London had to do with a Lacy's fashion show, and what any of it had to do with me.

"Anyway, Rex just called me with the most incredible opportunity. He's hosting the fashion show at Lacy's, and he's going to feature a bit of his fall collection. But primarily, it's going to be a preprofessional show for emerging talent. He's handpicked the absolute best of the best—the people who are going to be the next big thing—to each showcase one outfit on the runway. Except one of them just dropped out—something about a necessary move back to Europe or something, I'm not sure—and you know

Rex, he must have even numbers for perfect symmetry."

"Uh-huh . . ." Was Veronica really asking what I thought she was asking?

"Rex just called me to ask if I knew anyone fabulous who might be able to pop into his show at the last minute, and of course, I told him I knew the absolute best of the best: Katy Keene. I was shocked he hadn't found you himself already!"

"Well, I mean, how could he—it's not like I've ever shown my designs anywhere before—"

"I know, Katy, and that's a crime! It's time to change all that! So I told Rex *you'd* do his fashion show at Lacy's, and it's going to be the most amazing exposure for you. It's in less than two weeks, but I'm sure you're still sewing as quickly as ever. I assured him it wouldn't be a problem."

"Wow, Veronica. I don't even know what to say." What *could* I say? I was in such shock, I could barely string a sentence together! Me, exhibit one of my designs? In a real fashion show? At *Lacy's*?! This was like . . . the kind of once-in-a-lifetime, dreams-*do*-come-true moment that I thought only happened in the movies. Not in real life. Not to a girl who grew up in a fifth-floor walk-up apartment on Delancey Street.

Not to *me*.

"Say yes, silly!"

"Yes, of course, yes!" I closed my eyes and did a little happy dance. Unfortunately, when I opened them, an old woman with a tiny dog in her purse was looking at me like I'd lost it. "Sorry!" I whispered. "Life-changing opportunity!" I pointed at the phone. She seemed unimpressed.

"Katy?" Veronica asked.

"Yup, still here!" I did one more tiny happy dance. The woman with the dog would just have to deal. "Thank you! Thank you so much. Seriously, Veronica. You have no idea how much this means to me." That was the thing about V—it didn't matter that I hadn't spent much time with her recently. She was one of the most loyal people I'd ever met. "Thank you."

"No need to thank me. Just save me a front-row seat at Lacy's—and on Spring Street when you've got your very own show in Fashion Week."

Right now, that future didn't seem quite so far off. Who knew what could happen with this fashion show! A Lacy's buyer might want my designs. Or an investor might see the show and offer up seed money to get my line off the ground.

If nothing else, I'd see one of my designs go down the runway.

Mom would have loved this so much.

I said good-bye to Veronica and thanked her again, my mind already whirling in a thousand different directions. What was I going to make?! It had to be something *perfect*.

"Good news?"

I turned around. I'd been so distracted while talking to Veronica that I hadn't noticed that KO was now wearing the bleeding cactus sweater. And a pink suede fedora. And a dalmatian-printed silk scarf.

"The best." I burst out laughing, wrapping my arms around KO's waist. "The absolute best."

This really was going to be the most perfect fall ever!

CHAPTER SIX
Jorge

LOOK AT ME, I THOUGHT, flexing my right foot for the gods as I kicked up toward my ear, *I'm the king of New York.*

Some king. My jazz pants were easily three inches too short, and my brother Mateo's old NYPD T-shirt was easily two sizes too big. Even for someone jumping his way through *Newsies* choreography, I was serving less ragamuffin realness, and more disheveled diva on laundry day. I needed a wardrobe update, STAT. But the pittance I made slinging bacon-egg-and-cheeses at my family's bodega wasn't exactly keeping me in Capezio's finest.

Still, if I knew how to do anything, it was sell it. *Look at me.* I flashed my brightest smile at Jason Bravard as I pulled up into a piqué turn. It may have been just a class, but in the New York theatre world, and especially at Broadway Dance Center, there was no *just* anything. Jason Bravard taught Advanced Musical Theatre, but he was also a

Tony-winning choreographer. There was always a chance he'd stop the class, shouting, "You! The skinny Latinx kid who ripped the sleeves off his brother's old NYPD shirt so I couldn't see his pit stains! You're exactly who I need to star in my latest Broadway show!"

Okay, it wasn't a *big* chance, but it was still there.

The song ended, and that was the end of class. Wiping the sweat off my face with the bottom of my T-shirt, I followed the crowd of dancers toward the stack of bags slumped against the wall, hoping I'd remembered my water bottle.

"Hey. Jorge."

I turned, and Jason was beckoning me over. Me? Seriously?! I didn't even think he knew my name. Maybe this was my Puerto Rican Peggy Sawyer moment! I came into this class a youngster, but Jason Bravard could make me a star!

"You looked good out there." Jason crossed his arms, looking me over like I was an orange at Fairway he was considering buying. "Seriously good. This has been a strong summer for you. You're done with school now, right?"

"Yeah. I graduated this spring." Surreptitiously, I tried to dab at my forehead. I wished we could have had this conversation when I was a little less sweaty. That *Newsies* choreography did not mess around. You'd think they'd be too tired from delivering all those newspapers to jump so much, but apparently not.

"Working at all?"

"No." I was pretty sure he meant performing, not

flipping chopped cheeses for people on their lunch break. "I had planned to audition for stuff, but—"

"Summer's dead, anyway," he cut me off. "The real work starts now."

I nodded. Jason rubbed a hand over his salt-and-pepper beard, like he did when he was reading us for filth for messing up his choreography.

"I assume you heard about the *Hello, Dolly!* open call," he said eventually. "You and every other Suzy Q who just got off the bus from Wichita with a suitcase full of hair extensions and character shoes."

"Washington Heights is not Wichita," I retorted.

"You're a native?" He raised an eyebrow. "I should have recognized a fellow New Yorker. It's that city grit that helps you stick your landings."

Usually, all the city grit did was make my shoes look busted, but sure, let's say it helped me stick the landing.

"But unlike those Suzy Qs, I think you've got a real shot," Jason continued. Hope rose in my chest. If *Jason Bravard* thought I had a shot, then I actually might have a shot. In all the years I'd been coming here, I'd only ever heard him give one compliment, and it definitely hadn't been to me. "Get there early. It'll be a madhouse. But make sure you get seen. I'll tell Ethan to keep an eye out for you."

"You know Ethan Fox?"

"Oh yeah." Jason rolled his eyes affectionately. "We were at Juilliard together, back in his boy genius days, when I was just a run-of-the-mill hoofer."

Jason Bravard had definitely been a boy genius, too—I was pretty sure I remembered some story about him leaving school to choreograph the *On the Town* revival at Lincoln Center that went on to win a Tony—but I didn't want to be some kind of creepy fanboy who recited his own résumé back at him.

"I don't know what he's thinking with this *Hello, Dolly!* idea . . . I mean, don't get me wrong, *I* love me some old-school Broadway, but this is definitely not his thing," Jason mused. "But knowing Ethan, it'll be interesting. This could be your shot, Jorge," he said seriously. "And shots like this don't come around that often. Don't blow it."

"Thanks." I was pretty sure that was as close to an inspirational speech as I'd get from New York's most notoriously critical choreographer, so I'd take it.

The pressure was definitely on. As I walked into the entry hall, the chatter from the other dancers in class was about nothing but the Ethan Fox open call. I was pretty sure every aspiring actor in the city—and every aspiring actor who could get to the city—was going to be there. A good word from Jason Bravard might help me get noticed, but to really stand out, I'd have to *bring it*. Plus I'd need an absolutely perfect, career-defining audition look. Something that screamed "I'm the Barnaby of your dreams!" without being too costume-y.

There was only one person I could turn to.

I pulled my phone out of my pocket to text Katy Keene.

CHAPTER SEVEN
Pepper

I HAD NEVER CARED MUCH FOR MADELINE.

True, she pulled off a blunt bob, which is never easy, but all of that "two little girls in two straight lines" business gave me the willies. Plus, kind and considerate as Miss Clavel may have been, she was running a fairly bleak operation, what with all those tiny beds crammed into one room.

Me? I need my space.

No, I had never had any patience for Madeline. Eloise, however? Eloise was an icon. Even at six years old, she understood one of the most fundamental truths of existence: There is no better residence than a luxury hotel.

"Welcome to the Five Seasons Hotel New York." The concierge's smile was as cool as her ice-blonde hair, smooth and pulled into an elegant French twist. Understated pearls gleamed on her earlobes, and a silk scarf was tied in an elegant knot around her neck. The Five Seasons may have been old-school, but every bit of the operation was pure class. "How may I be of assistance?"

"I do hope you can help me." I answered the concierge's smile with a cool one of my own. "I believe the reservation is under my father's name, but he's been unavoidably detained in Hong Kong on business. The rainy season, you know. Absolute murder on the international market."

"Of course, Miss Smith." Even with my enormous cat's-eye sunglasses, she'd recognized me. It couldn't be helped. Then again, I'd never understood those LA actors who wandered through the airport in their grubby baseball caps and hooded sweatshirts. If one was going to be incognito, one should at least do it with style. "I believe we have a card on file for any incidental charges, under the name P. Smith. Is that the card you'd like to use?"

I nodded, smiling as I remembered some of my school chums, who had had access to their daddies' credit cards "in case of emergencies." Silly girls. The only proof against emergency was to have unrestricted access to a healthy line of credit.

"I do hope I'll be able to check in early?"

"Of course, Miss Smith. We have you in the Luna Suite. I hope that will be satisfactory."

"More than satisfactory." It wasn't the largest suite in the Five Seasons, but it had a lovely view of the park. Besides, my dear friends—more like a beloved aunt and uncle, really—Michelle and Barack were currently in residence in the largest suite for a much-needed getaway, and lord knew they deserved the Presidential Suite far more than I did.

"I hope you'll be able to relax here in New York, given your recent . . ." I watched her look for a word, fail, and then eventually settle on "situation."

Ah, that pesky royal affair. This had been one of the most persistent rumors to dog my heels in recent memory. It was rare for a rumor to follow me across the Atlantic, and even rarer for one to pop up like this, so completely unexpectedly and without my knowledge. Of course, one only had so much control over one's press, but usually I at least had *some* idea of what was going to be said about me and where it was coming from. Especially if it was as wildly untrue as this.

The royals. Only a lunatic or a fool would try to throw their lot in with that band of rascals. The tabloids had been so oblique, I couldn't even fathom whom I was meant to have seduced. Breaking up a marriage was not my style, nor was attempting to worm my way into a family situation that required its women to be permanently panty hosed. I was happy to have my bare legs firmly planted on American soil, thank you very much.

Silently, a bellhop glided over to take my bags as the concierge slid my room key across the desk. The very air in here felt better than it did anywhere else: cool and lightly floral. With each inhale, I felt like I could breathe a little easier.

It was good to be home.

CHAPTER EIGHT
Josie

I'LL SAY THIS MUCH FOR Comfort Motel corporate—
they had the whole formula down to a science. I'd lost
track of how many we'd stayed in, but no matter what
state we were in, each motel had been exactly the same.
Each lobby boasted blue couches with pop-of-color orange
throw pillows, a big dark wood reception desk with a
white counter, and a breakfast buffet off to the side, where
I knew the same chafing dish of rubbery scrambled eggs,
tiny yogurts, and individual packets of oatmeal would be
waiting for me in the morning. If I was really lucky, there'd
be a mixed-berry yogurt and a maple-and-brown-sugar
oatmeal, instead of just blueberry and plain.

Oof, Josie. I shook my head. I should not be getting this
excited about mixed-berry yogurt. I was pretty sure
Beyoncé never stepped off her tour bus dreaming about
yogurt flavors. She had bigger things on her mind, like

world domination. And that was exactly what I needed to keep at the top of my mind, too.

But first, snacks. We'd finished another great show at the Stranahan Theater about an hour ago, and I was starving. Our hotel was in a parking lot just off the highway, the better to hit the road bright and early in the morning, but it wasn't so great for the late-night dining options. There was nothing around us, not even the neon lights of a fast-food joint or a gas station with a nice big chip selection. And, of course, Dad had insisted we come right to the motel after the show, no stopping for food allowed. So there was only one option. But if the Comfort Motel Toledo was exactly like all the rest, the vending machine would be down the hall and past the elevators, tucked into a nook by the ice machine. And of course, it was. In a world full of uncertainty, at least these Comfort Motels were reliable.

Archie Andrews stood in front of the vending machine.

I stumbled, my black cage booties practically folding under me as my ankles buckled.

Catching my breath, I took a second look, and it wasn't him. Of course it wasn't him—there was absolutely no reason for Archie to be at a Comfort Motel in Toledo. I rested a hand against the taupe-colored wall, steadying myself. Taking a better look at the stranger, he really didn't look that much like Archie at all. For one thing, his hair wasn't red. It was a light, burnished brown, shining a little golden even under the fluorescent lights. But there was something about the way he was standing and the set of his broad shoulders that made me think about Archie. Maybe it was because he was wearing a Henley.

Or maybe it was because of the acoustic guitar strapped to his back.

Suddenly, I was back in the Riverdale High music room again, sitting on a wooden bench in front of that janky old keyboard, telling Archie I was leaving. I could still feel the gentle kiss he'd pressed on my forehead. In a town that was anything but sweet and uncomplicated, somehow Archie still managed to be both of those things. We may not have been endgame, but there was no doubt that Archie Andrews was one of the good ones.

And now, here I was. Somewhere out there, just like I told Archie I would be. No wonder I'd been rocked back on my heels by this stranger with the guitar. It felt like I'd seen a ghost. Like if I tried to touch him, my hand would pass right through.

The stranger reached up, tall enough that he could drum his fingers on top of the vending machine. He leaned against it as his fingers continued to drum, staring into the depths of the machine like he was searching for answers.

"What to pick," he murmured, so low I could barely make out the words. Or, at least, I think that's what he said. "What. To. Pick."

I coughed, once, just in case he hadn't heard me come up behind him.

"Hmmm," he hummed, still drumming his fingers.

I coughed again. Still, he didn't move.

Okay, I understood the importance of choosing the right snack, but this was getting ridiculous. Plus that drumming was working my last nerve. I tapped my foot, but the sound was completely muffled by the carpet.

"Easy there, darlin'," he said without turning around. His voice was low, and the vowels long and smooth. He certainly didn't sound like the boys back home in Riverdale. "Don't wanna wear a hole in the carpet with those pretty shoes."

"Ooh, honey, I think you've miscalculated," I said tartly. "You don't have a 'darlin'' in this hallway."

"Is that right." I could hear the smile in his voice before he turned around, and when he hit me with the full force of it, it was killer. It was the kind of white, even smile that could have beamed out of a thousand middle school girls' lockers. He wasn't famous—at least, I didn't think he was—but he looked like he could be, someday. He rubbed his stubbled jaw with one large hand, then looked me up and down. Suddenly I felt conscious of the short length of my black bandage dress. My fingers itched to tug the hem downward, but I didn't want to give him the satisfaction of knowing that I'd noticed him looking at my legs. "You look too good not to be somebody's darlin'."

"Does that sexism come standard issue with the tight jeans in whatever pickle barrel of a small Southern town you crawled out of, country boy?"

He burst out laughing.

"I'm not from a pickle barrel, Josie McCoy. I'm from Nashville. Music City."

"How do you know my name?" My eyes narrowed as I tried to judge whether or not he was dangerous, and if I'd be able to outrun him into the lobby to call for help. Even hotties could be stalkers.

"Caught the show tonight. You've got quite a voice. I'm Boone Wyant." He stuck out his hand. Reluctantly, I shook it, still trying to figure out if he was a normal fan, or if he'd followed me back here. "I'm playing the Stranahan tomorrow night."

He was playing our venue. Was he a . . . country singer? He must have been. It was hard to imagine Boone Wyant, with his cowboy boots and guitar, singing anything else. Even his name sounded country.

"So you're not stalking me?" I raised an eyebrow.

"Not yet." He grinned. "I mean, no, ma'am, I'm not stalking you. Shouldn't joke about that. Sorry."

"I like *ma'am* even less than I like *darlin'*."

"Boy, I'm striking out on all counts tonight, aren't I?" He rubbed his hand over his jaw again. Some guys were built for stubble, and Boone Wyant was one of them. "Let me start over. Please. Hey there. I'm Boone Wyant." He smiled at me, and I found myself smiling back at him, almost in spite of myself. "I loved the show tonight. I've been a big fan of your daddy's for some time, and I've never heard a voice quite like yours. You've really got something."

"Josie McCoy. Nice to meet you," I said. "You're really a Myles McCoy fan?"

"Even country boys can like jazz." We stood there for a moment in the hallway, smiling at each other. I wasn't totally convinced he wasn't a sexist dingbat, but I had to admit, the boy had charisma. "I gotta say, I'm not feeling anything in this vending machine. You wanna go get some real food, Josie McCoy?"

There wasn't a clock in this corner of the hallway, but I knew it had to be pushing midnight. I didn't technically have a curfew, or check-in, or anything like that, but I had a feeling that was just because Dad assumed I'd be tucked up in bed as soon as we checked in, resting my voice before the next night.

"You know what?" My eyes lingered on his shoulders, and the way they filled out that Henley like it had been custom-made for him. "I do, Boone Wyant. I really, really do."

CHAPTER NINE
Katy

THE FIRST TIME JORGE AND I snuck into Molly's Crisis, we literally snuck in. We were only fourteen, and in an attempt to look older, we were both wearing so much makeup it looked like we had tried to smuggle an entire Sephora's worth of testers out of the store on our faces. (Which, to be fair, wasn't that far off from the truth. In high school, we'd become the world's fastest makeup artists, giving each other fully executed looks before the sales clerks could come over to investigate why we'd tried every product in the store but never bought anything.) I think, if I'm remembering correctly, Jorge had even spirit-gummed a full beard onto his face? Which was a totally different color from his eyebrows. But his eye makeup had been so gorgeous, I'm sure no one would have noticed his beard. If anyone had been looking at us. Which, luckily, they weren't.

Molly's Crisis is a dive bar that features a constantly

rotating carousel of drag performers. And the very first time Jorge and I had snuck in, it had been Dolly Parton night. The place had been packed to bursting with busty blonde queens, and no one had noticed two overly made-up teenagers slipping in among the rhinestones and fringe. We'd huddled in the back of the bar, too afraid of getting kicked out to even order a soda, transported by what we'd seen. Before the first queen had even finished the first verse of "Jolene," Jorge and I were in love. The costumes, the makeup, the music . . . everything about it was wonderful. I'd never been in a room full of so many people just having *fun*.

We kept coming back, and by the time someone noticed that we were definitely too young to be there, the softhearted manager figured that as long as we didn't try to order any alcohol, we weren't bothering anybody. We grew up alongside Judy and Barbra and Liza, and our makeup had definitely improved because of it.

True, the floors were sticky, the soda was usually flat, and the queens could sometimes be a little pitchy, but Molly's Crisis was home. It was our escape from reality, into a world of glitter and laughter and fun, and after the last couple of years, Jorge and I had certainly needed to escape a time or two.

"More Cherry Coke, Katy Keene?" Darius asked, holding up the soda gun like Charlie's lost Angel. With his blond feathered wig, he could certainly give Farrah Fawcett a run for her money.

"Yes, please." I pushed my glass across the bar toward him. "I need all the caffeine and sugar I can get."

Before things really got hopping, Molly's Crisis was a surprisingly good place to work. The light was a little dim, but not so much that I couldn't see, and they used nice warm lightbulbs. Plus the soundtrack of '80s and '90s hits made me feel like I was working with Mom, who never met a pop song she didn't love to sew to. Right now, it was just me and my sketchbook at the bar. A couple performers in half drag sat at one of the tables, quietly going over notes before tonight's show. I hoped I'd get enough work done so that I could stay and see their number before heading to the Starlite to meet KO for a late dinner. I'd heard something about Beyoncé, and a little inspiration from Queen Bey sounded like exactly what I needed.

"Easy on the caffeine. You'll stunt your growth, Lil Bit." Despite his warning, Darius filled my glass up to the brim with soda, and tossed in a few extra maraschino cherries, since he knew how much I loved them.

"I'm eighteen. I think that ship has sailed. I have made my peace with being five foot two and the proud owner of *several* pairs of heels, thank you very much."

"Ooh, *several*, huh? Then let's see 'em, fancy lady." Darius crooked a finger and waggled it at me until I swung around on the barstool and plopped my left foot up on the bar. Luckily, I was wearing a cute pair tonight, one of my favorites. They had bright red stacked heels, sturdy enough to stand up to even the cobblestones in the Village, with navy sides and a rounded toe. I'd found the shoes in a vintage store on the Lower East Side, then cut up an old red leather purse to create heart details I super-glued on the toes, giving the shoes a bit more Katy personality. I could never resist adding a good heart detail, especially one in my favorite color.

"Did they start the floor show early?" I smiled at the sound of my best friend's voice, a burst of cool air following him in as the door shut behind him. "I didn't know you were performing tonight, Katy." Jorge walked into the bar, the rhinestones on his cropped, teal, off-the-shoulder sweatshirt catching the light. I loved that sweatshirt. Jorge had found it at a thrift store, and then we'd cut it and bedazzled it together while singing along to *Fame* until my next-door neighbor pounded on the wall to get us to shut up.

"Yes, please stay for my show, 'Girl Sits Alone at Bar with Sketchbook,'" I deadpanned. "Critics have called it 'very boring.'"

"Can't wait." Jorge winked.

"Well. If it isn't the coldest boy in cold town," Darius said flatly. "Should I get him a glass of pure ice?"

"Excuse *me*. What did I do to deserve this shade?" Jorge deposited a quick kiss on top of my head, then slid onto the barstool next to me.

"'What did I do?'" Darius repeated with disbelief. "'What did I do?' he asks. 'What did I *do*?!'"

"Wait a minute." Jorge smacked his forehead. "Darius, you are unreal. Is this still about Whitney?"

"'Is this still about Whitney?' he asks," Darius muttered, before he did, in fact, place a glass of ice in front of Jorge, a pink cocktail umbrella resting jauntily on the rim. "'Is this *still* about *Whitney*?!'"

"Can you stop repeating everything I say with a different em*pha*sis?" Jorge asked, sticking the umbrella behind his ear. "And can I get some ginger ale in this glass, chillona, or are you too busy being petty?"

"Who's Whitney?" I asked.

"'Who's Whitney?'" Darius repeated. "'*Who's Whitney?!*' The *youth* today! They don't know the culture!"

"Katy knows who Whitney Houston is," Jorge scoffed.

"Oh, yeah, of course." I nodded. "I just thought you guys were talking about, like, a friend named Whitney."

"I don't have any friends named Whitney." Brandishing the soda gun with a flourish, Darius filled Jorge's glass with ginger ale.

"He's mad about Whitney Houston," Jorge explained. "I stopped by for Whitney Wednesday and apparently I disappointed him."

"When this bar plays 'I Wanna Dance With Somebody,' you do not disrespect Whitney by *not dancing*," Darius said seriously. "Especially since I *asked you* to dance, and I had been bragging about you to my friends—"

"Friends who are not named Whitney," I interjected.

"And I expected you to *bring it*!"

"I was dancing!" Jorge protested.

"You were dancing like a white boy at his cousin's wedding." Darius snorted.

"How many white boy weddings have you been to?" Jorge arched a perfectly plucked eyebrow.

"You were dancing like a white boy at his cousin's wedding in *Connecticut*." Darius smacked the bar for emphasis.

"Ooh, now you've taken it too far, bish." Jorge mimed taking off pretend earrings. "I'm gonna have to fight you."

"What's wrong with Connecticut?" I asked.

"Girl, I'm not the kind of magical as-seen-on-TV drag queen who educates little straight girls for fun. Figure it out. And as for you." Darius turned to Jorge with a look. "I wanted to see the real stuff," he complained. "Jumps, leaps, twirls, turns, death drops, all that business."

"I'm not doing any of that on this sticky cement floor." Jorge shook his head. "It's like you *want* me to bust my knees up."

"Jorge. I've seen you leap off this bar and drop into a split onto that exact sticky cement floor." He tapped the bar for emphasis. "Is that a move that only Robyn gets, or . . ."

"I'm trying to be a responsible, adult-type person!" Jorge threw up his hands in exasperation. "I have the biggest audition of my *life* tomorrow, and I'm not going to mess that up for Whitney Wednesday!"

"Is that why you wanted to meet to talk about clothes?" I interrupted, flipping my sketchbook closed and pushing it to the side excitedly. I knew how disappointed Jorge had been about not getting cast in anything this summer, and I'd hated seeing him all aimless, like a pale copy of my normally vibrant friend. "You got an audition?"

"Yes!" Jorge grabbed my hands in his. I loved seeing how fired up he was. I knew being home with his parents had been taking a toll on him, and I was so happy to see him looking more like his usual self. "And it's not just any audition. It's *the* audition. It's an open call, for an Ethan Fox–directed Broadway production of *Hello, Dolly!*, and there's a part that is *perfect* for me."

"*Hello, Dolly!*?" Darius snorted. "'Beneath your parasol the world is all a smile,' *Hello, Dolly!*? You couldn't get me into a pair of those high-button shoes for love or money. That show is cheesier than Velveeta."

"It won't be cheesy if Ethan Fox is directing it," Jorge shot back. "And don't you have inventory to go over before it gets busy tonight?"

"Stop trying to do my job!" Darius threw up his hands.

"Actually . . . maybe I should do your job," Jorge mused. "Now that I'm eighteen, I can legally bartend. Darius, can I work here? Will you train me?"

"Girl, I don't have time to teach babies how to mix martinis—"

"Has anyone here ever ordered a *martini*?" I asked. Molly's Crisis had more of a tequila shot vibe.

"I have inventory to do!" Darius turned toward the

storeroom. "Katy, don't leave without my jumpsuit," he called behind him. "There's a little tear near the shoulders I need you to fix. And some missing rhinestones."

"On it!" I shouted. He waved in response before turning his attention to the shelves of bottles. "An audition, Jorge? This is so exciting!" I squeezed my best friend's hands. "I'm so happy for you. I know you're going to crush this. You're so talented, and this Ethan Fish person will be *begging* to cast you."

"Fox," Jorge corrected.

"Right, yes, Fox, sorry," I apologized. "So . . . the outfit?"

"Yes. Okay. So, for the open call, it's just sixteen bars of a classic musical theatre song," Jorge said. "No sides, no monologue, and no dance call, so I don't need to worry about movement. The dance call will be at callbacks, if I make it."

"*When* you make it," I corrected him.

"When," he agreed, smiling. "And I'll obviously wear my lucky green shorts for the dance call."

"Obviously," I agreed.

"You know I was wearing those shorts when I made out with—"

"Chase Peterman-Yang right after he played Prince Eric at theatre camp," we finished together. It was not the first time I'd heard the story of Chase Peterman-Yang and the in-costume Prince Eric make-out.

If only Jorge hadn't been dressed as Flounder, it would have been a romantic moment for the ages.

"It was a perfect summer," Jorge said wistfully. "Except *I* should have been Ariel. That girl did *not* have the range. And, hello, this body was made for a tail." Jorge encircled his petite waist with his hands and posed like Ariel singing on the rock.

"But *Hello, Dolly!*?" I prompted him.

"Right. So I want to look sort of period-suggestive, but not costume-y, you know? Like, I'm serving you Yonkers. I'm serving you the late nineteenth century. But I'm not serving you tuberculosis, you feel me?"

"Got it. Although, not quite totally sure what about a look screams 'Yonkers,'" I mused, flipping open my sketchbook.

"Get out the Brilliantine and dime cigars!" Darius sang from the back.

"Can *you* get out?" Jorge shouted back. "No Brilliantine necessary!"

Laughing, I flipped past the dress I was working on to a clean sheet of paper.

"Hey, wait a minute." Jorge grabbed my hand and flipped back to the dress. "What are you doodling, Katy Keene? This is gorgeous. Is this for your Parsons application?"

"Oh no." I brushed his hand off and turned the page, smoothing the fresh sheet. "You know that's on pause. Indefinitely. Maybe forever."

"Katy-girl." Jorge reached out and tapped on the back of my hand with his index finger. "Not forever. Parsons is your dream school."

"It was Mom's dream, too," I said softly. I blinked as I looked down at the sketchbook, the page blurring as my eyes filled with tears. I had always planned to go to Parsons School of Design after high school, so I could study fashion and then launch my career as a designer, like famous alumni Anna Sui and Marc Jacobs and Donna Karan. Mom and I had been talking about my Parsons application since preschool, practically.

But then she had gotten sick, and it had taken all my effort just to get through high school and graduate. I hadn't put together a portfolio for my application, and even with health insurance, there wasn't exactly a lot of money left over, what with the hospital bills and Mom having to close her store.

I didn't have any regrets about how I'd spent senior year. I would never regret a single moment I'd spent with Mom. She had been my priority, as she should have been. It just meant there hadn't been any time for Parsons.

"She'd want you to go, Katy," Jorge urged me. He sounded so certain that this was the right thing to do, that it would definitely happen for me. "She'd want you to at least apply. You've been dreaming of this for so long."

"Maybe next year," I said, although I wasn't so sure. Being at Parsons without Mom there to see it seemed almost more painful than not going at all. I already thought of things I wanted to tell her about a million times a day. How could I handle doing something we'd dreamed of together for so long without being able to share it with her?

"Yes, next year for sure. But if it's not for Parsons, what's the dress for? Nothing that gorgeous should just be theoretical."

"Well, it's not for Parsons, but it is for something pretty exciting. Maybe even *more* exciting." I wasn't sure where Lacy's and Parsons would fall on a list of "Katy's Favorite Things." It would be like choosing between my red coat with the Peter Pan collar and my heart-shaped clutch. Impossible! "Rex London is hosting a fashion show for emerging designers at Lacy's. And *I'm* one of those emerging designers!"

"Rex London? Like from-TV Rex London? Hosting a fashion show? At *Lacy's*?!" I was nodding so vigorously I felt like a bobblehead. A dopey, ecstatic, grinning bobblehead. "Oh, Katy!" Jorge pulled me into a hug so enthusiastic I slid off the barstool a little. "This is your big break! At your favorite store in the world! And Rex London is really hot!"

The relative hotness of Rex London had never even entered my mind, but the man certainly knew how to wear a suit. I filled Jorge in on everything I knew so far. I'd gotten all the details on the fashion show in an email from Rex London's assistant mere moments after Veronica had hung up. She was almost scary-efficient. I had no doubt Veronica would be running all of Lodge Industries—maybe all of the world—in no time at all.

"Girl, I can see it now." Jorge held up his hands like he was a director framing a shot. "Mrs. Lacy herself will fall so in love with your designs at the fashion show, she'll throw a ton of money at you to start your own line, and by next fall, *everyone* will be wearing a Katy Keene original."

"Maybe." It was unlikely, but it was hard not to get swept up in the excitement and the possibility. "Honestly, I don't even need my own line. Right now, I'd take *any* job at Lacy's. But they're not hiring. Not even in the stockroom."

"Honey, the stockroom? You're too cute to be tucked away back there." Jorge frowned. "Let's just focus on you becoming a rich and famous designer. Now, tell me about your dress."

"Well . . . this was what I was thinking." I flipped back to the page I'd been sketching on. "The silhouette is almost a little '40s, with the strong shoulder and the narrow waist. But not, you know, too costume-y. But I don't know . . . something doesn't feel quite right . . ."

"Seriously?" Jorge's brow furrowed. "I love it. I mean, *I'd* wear it. But of course, the most important thing is that it feels right to *you*."

"Yeah." I tucked a piece of hair behind my ears, smoothing it down, like that might help me smooth my frazzled thoughts. "I don't know. I need to start sewing right away—I've got less than two weeks until the fashion show—but I just don't know if this design is *enough*. This dress needs to be perfect. I only get to show one look, and that's what Rex London—and everyone at Lacy's, and anyone else in the fashion world who comes—will see me as. This is it. My one shot. I can't mess it up."

"Katy-girl, you are not throwing away your shot, and neither am I."

"Oh my god, right! We're not supposed to be talking about me; we're talking about *you*." I flipped over to a clean sheet of paper. "What about a Henley?" I started sketching, the lines of Jorge's shoulders coming to life on the page. "Suspenders might be too much, but a Henley feels kind of late-nineteenth-century-stock-boy suggestive. You could pair it with your brown pants and leather boots."

"This could work." Jorge leaned over my shoulder, watching as the sketch took form. "Not gonna lie, I kind of *want* to wear suspenders . . ."

"I'm certainly not going to stop you. Life needs more suspenders moments." My phone vibrated on the bar. I picked it up—a text from KO.

"Lover boy?" Jorge asked. "What's the handsome heavyweight up to?"

"He's training." I clicked open the text. "We were supposed to meet for dinner at the Starlite after, but he just texted me to cancel. He's got this new sparring partner and apparently they're in a real groove."

"Well, we certainly wouldn't want to mess up a boxing groove." Jorge smiled. "More time for me to have you all to myself."

I smiled back. Of course, I was always happy for more time with Jorge, and a little more sketching time certainly wouldn't hurt, but it wasn't like KO to cancel plans. Still, I shouldn't be selfish. I'd been leaning on him so much recently, and I always wanted him to know that I supported his boxing, just like he supported all my dreams.

"Let's stay for the show," I said. "Maybe a little Beyoncé is exactly what I need to get this dress right."

I turned back to the page and looked down at my dress. What was wrong with it? Well, there was nothing *wrong* with it exactly. But maybe that wasn't the problem. There wasn't enough *right* with it. I'd liked it at first, but the more I looked at it, the less special it was. Maybe I should start over. Maybe I shouldn't do a dress at all. Would a jumpsuit be better? Or something that showed off my tailoring?

Since I was a replacement, I'd have less time to work on whatever I ended up presenting than everyone else had. They'd already probably finished their designs. They may even have finished sewing and were just doing adjustments. The timeline was so tight. How could I ever come up with the perfect thing before the show?

I wished I could show it to Mom. She'd know exactly what to do. Even when a design was just a sketch, she could tell, instantly, whether the skirt would hang strangely, or if a hemline would hit awkwardly. She had a sixth sense for seeing something and knowing whether or not it would be magic on the hanger. I wished I had that gift.

No, I just wished I had Mom.

"If you stay for Beyoncé, and you don't dance when

those horns come in for 'Crazy in Love,' I'll kick you out of this bar *myself*!" Darius appeared from the back, a bottle of something bright blue in his hands. "I haven't forgotten that y'all aren't twenty-one yet!"

Jorge ignored him and looked at me, his warm brown eyes serious.

"Katy-girl. The dress is good. *You* are good. No matter what you make, your talent will shine through. Don't overthink it." He ruffled my hair, like he was trying to shake all the thoughts out of my brain. I wished it was that easy, but it wasn't.

How could I not overthink it?

One dress.

One shot.

It had to be *perfect*.

CHAPTER TEN
Jorge

IT WAS WORSE THAN I'D THOUGHT.

Usually most auditions were at the Pearl or Ripley-Grier, two buildings with endless warrens of audition rooms and studio spaces, or at the Equity Building. Even if you weren't Equity, you could wait in the hallway for a chance to be seen, but as I learned the first time, the chances of that were slim, and you weren't allowed to use the bathroom. The privilege of peeing was reserved for Equity members only. As I'd waited in that line, I'd remembered the minor riot that had broken out in New York a couple years ago when the girls waiting to audition for *America's Next Super Model* had gotten into a scuffle about holding places in line to find a bathroom.

Hopefully, there wouldn't be any riots in the *Hello, Dolly!* open call line. They were holding the auditions downtown at the Private Theatre, a well-respected venue that had workshopped a lot of new musicals before they transferred to Broadway, and that ran free Shakespeare in the Park every summer. Ethan Fox had come up at the Private, so it wasn't a surprise that he'd be starting out *Hello, Dolly!* here, too.

It was 7:00 a.m. and the auditions weren't scheduled to start until 11:00, but the line was already down the block. I shuffled into place behind a clean-cut white guy my age with brown hair. He looked like a Ken doll, or like a propaganda poster from World War II celebrating the vitality of the all-American boy. But he was working it.

Some people chatted in line, but like many a reality TV beeyatch before me, I wasn't here to make friends. I popped my headphones on and listened to a playlist I'd made of nothing but Broadway overtures, hoping the instrumental music would keep me calm. The line continued to fill in behind me, and by 9:00 a.m., it had wrapped around the block.

By 10:00 a.m., the news vans showed up.

"Unreal," I muttered. Just like the *Hair* open call I'd seen with Ma when I was little. Not surprisingly, the news vans went straight for the people who'd showed up in full costume, a move I *never* understood. And, like, if you're gonna come in costume, don't be so sloppy. It looked like Party City had held a going-out-of-business sale—buy two hideous hats and we'll throw in a dented parasol for free. All the queens at Molly's would have been *horrified* by how much straight-up busted was on display.

Finally, at 11:00, the doors opened. I was far enough away that I didn't move at all, but a ripple of excitement moved down the line regardless.

We were moving so slowly it was *killing me.* I hadn't been part of anything this painful since Darius tried to hit the whistle tones while testing out a Mariah act. No tea no shade, D could always work it, but Mariah was in a league of her own. Kind of like the hottie in front of me. Every once in a while, I'd catch a snatch of All-American Boy vocalizing in front of me. He sounded good. Really good. But I'd just have to block him, and the rest of my competition, out.

After seemingly endless hours, I finally made it inside. Where, of course, I waited some more. Finally, at the end of the hall, a monitor stood with a clipboard. She took my name and a copy of my headshot, and directed All-American Boy into the room. Only minutes later, he was back out. I tried to read his face for signs of confidence or disappointment, but he still looked blandly pleasant, like he was about to model knit wool beanies in a J.Crew catalog. Maybe he was. He had great bone structure.

"You're up," the monitor said, nodding at me. "Break a leg."

I nodded back at her, then walked into a small black box theater. Everything was black, from the walls to the floor to the seats in the audience. There was a black piano in the middle of the room, the black paint on the floor scratched to reveal wood underneath from where it had been moved. A bald, older man with glasses sat at the piano, his hands poised expectantly at the keys. Behind a table at the front of the audience, there were three men and a woman. And one of those men was Ethan Fox.

Oh my god. I'd assumed they'd be running multiple audition rooms with different casting people, that we'd have to clear who knew how many hurdles before we saw the man himself, but there he was. I shook off my shock, smiling in a way that hopefully looked friendly and professional.

They want *it to be you.* That was what Ma had said before every audition in school. *Remember, m'hijo, they are waiting there, hoping* you *will be the one to solve their problem. To be exactly what they're looking for. Sing for them like you know that they want it to be you.*

"Jorge Lopez," I introduced myself, dropping four copies of my headshot and résumé on the table in front of them. A more intense version of me brooded back up from the headshot. I probably shouldn't have taken those pictures when I'd been feeling so dramatic, but oh well.

"Jorge! From Jason's class." *Ethan Fox knew my name.* I glued my smile into place to keep my jaw from dropping open. "Jason says this kid can really dance," Ethan addressed the other people at the table.

"Then let's hope he can really sing," the woman said, flipping my headshot over to look at my résumé. I winced slightly, hoping it wouldn't immediately disqualify me that I only had school credits, nothing professional. But everybody has to start somewhere, right? "Jorge, what do you have for us today?"

"'All I Need Is the Girl,' from *Gypsy*," I said. Which, LOL, I never needed a girl, but the song was right in my range. I walked over to the piano and handed my sheet music to the pianist. He spread it out. I'd brought the whole song, even though I knew I'd only get sixteen bars. Wishful thinking, maybe?

"Tempo?" he asked.

I hummed the first bar, tapping my foot to the rhythm I wanted. He nodded and turned back to the sheet music.

"Ready whenever you are, Jorge," Ethan said.

Breathe. Don't forget to breathe. Right. Breathing was very important. It was just me and the piano and this room.

And a panel of judgmental, unsmiling people who would decide my fate, but, you know. No pressure.

The pianist started, a little faster than I'd hoped, but that had probably been my fault. The nerves must have made me tap too quickly. And just like that, the intro was over, I took a deep breath, and I sang.

I sounded good. Really good. Everything flowed easily, the sound filling the black box. I searched their faces for signs that I was crushing it like I thought I was, but it was like looking at a brick wall. In just a few heartbeats, it was over.

Sixteen bars was nothing. I couldn't believe how long I'd waited, just for the chance to sing for less than a minute— in the hopes that I'd impressed them enough for them to want to see me again. And there were *so many people* willing to do that.

Well, this business was something else, and you had to be a few bristles short of a makeup brush to want to be part of it.

"Great, thanks." They weren't smiling exactly, but they weren't frowning, either. "We'll definitely want to see you for the dance call," Ethan said, and I exhaled so forcefully, with such relief, I was surprised it didn't knock the pianist over. "Does tomorrow at six p.m. work for you for callbacks?"

"That works." I could be there at six p.m. Six a.m. Four a.m. Anytime! Ethan Fox wanted me to come to the dance call! I'd dance on a subway grate if he needed me to! On the sidewalk on trash pickup day! I'd even dance in *Long Island*!

This could happen. This could actually happen.

No, this *would* happen.

I picked up my sheet music and thanked everyone, my heart soaring. Now, all I had to do was dance.

And nobody danced like me.

CHAPTER ELEVEN
Pepper

Transcript from *Let's Give 'Em Something to Pod About,* Episode 85

CHLOE: Welcome to *Let's Give 'Em Something to Pod About,* your source for everything you need to know about every*one* you need to know, here in the only city worth knowing about. I'm your host, Chloe van Sant, and we have an *unbelievable* guest here today. But first, a word from our sponsors.

Using the code PodAbout, get your first Wow Well Whee! box for only $29.99. Every month, the folks at Wow Well Whee! will send you an *amazing* box of curated products, the best of the wellness and beauty worlds. Each box has over $200 worth of luxury items, for only $39.99, except you, my dear Podlettes, get your first one for only $29.99! This month, I'm loving my cashmere lounge socks, my sea buckthorn facial spray, and an absolutely *amaze* tomato leaf–scented candle that will *transport* you to fields of Tuscany or your grandma's garden or whatever. Get a taste of the *Pod About* luxury life with Wow Well Whee!

And, back to the main event. I am absolutely *thrilled* to welcome our guest here for her very first time on the pod. You know her, you love her, you can't get enough of her. It's the one, the only, Pepper Smith!

PEPPER: Cheers, Chloe. Thanks for having me.

CHLOE: Oh my god, the accent. I can't. It's just too cute.

PEPPER: *You're* the one with the cute accent.

CHLOE: Stop. Podlettes, can you even with her? Pepper, we are so lucky to have you back in New York.

PEPPER: I love New York. The energy, the people, there's always something happening . . .

CHLOE: Do I detect some subtle shade at our neighbors across the pond?

PEPPER: Not at all, Chloe. London is just a very different city. It's apple pie and chocolate oranges.

CHLOE: Cute. So your departure from the mother country *did* have something to do with a certain *swoon*-worthy royal romance?

PEPPER: Ah, Chloe, you mustn't believe everything you read in the tabloids. I've never been one for dwelling in the past. I'm much more interested in what happens next.

CHLOE: Message received. And I think we're all *very* interested in what happens next. What's the plan here in New York?

PEPPER: Fall in New York is exquisite, isn't it? I'm so pleased to be here for Fashion Week, one of my favorite times of the year.

CHLOE: No surprise there. Podlettes, I wish you could see this jumpsuit—the wide legs, the deep V, the sunny yellow shade. It's to die for. I'll be sure to post it on our Insta—give us a follow @PodAbout. So Pepper, any shows you're particularly excited for?

PEPPER: I'm actually most excited for something that's not part of the official Fashion Week lineup.

CHLOE: Of course you are! Trust Pepper Smith to have the underground scoop!

PEPPER: This year, Rex London is hosting—

CHLOE: Rex London?! Oh-em-gee, *obsessed.* I live for his show.

PEPPER: Yes, Rex is a wonderful man, and a dear friend. And I'm so excited to share that—

CHLOE: Is this an exclusive scoop for the pod?

PEPPER: Erm, I'm not Rex London's press secretary, so I couldn't rightly say. But this year, Rex London is hosting a fashion show at Lacy's—

CHLOE: A fashion show? Inside a department store? What *will* the man think of next?

PEPPER: Yes, a fashion show that features new and upcoming designers, ones whose work has *never* previously been exhibited before. It can be so hard to find truly innovative designs from established labels. Recently, I've been finding my best looks come from designers no one has ever heard of before.

CHLOE: Is that where you found this jumpsuit? Give us the deets, girl!

PEPPER: Ah, no, this was a gift from my dear friend Clare. Even an older, established design house like Givenchy can sometimes have a few tricks up its sleeve.

CHLOE: Pepper, *you* have such style. I mean, seriously, your Instagram? I'm obsessed! Have you ever thought of designing?

PEPPER: Goodness, no. I prefer to lend my support to those artists who are truly gifted. Perhaps that's what I truly wish to do here in New York—create a space where others can, well, create.

CHLOE: You heard it here on the pod first, folks. Pepper Smith, benefactress of the arts, is here to help New Yorkers get artsy! We'll be back with some more questions for Pepper about what's going on in her love life now, but first, another word from Wow Well Whee! Have I told you guys about the tomato leaf candle? It's life changing!

CHAPTER TWELVE
Josie

"YOU TAKE ALL THE GIRLS to truck stops?" I asked Boone.

"Only the really special ones." He winked.

I opened the giant menu, the pages laminated and sticky. Almost as sticky as the floor. I lifted my heels, feeling suction as I pulled up off the black-and-white tile. A tired-looking waitress passed us, a coffeepot in each hand and multiple pens stuck into her hair. For a minute, with the clink of silverware and the smell of coffee in the air, it was almost like being back at Pop's.

I didn't miss Riverdale, not exactly, but my mind kept going back to Pop's. Maybe what I was missing was being around friends. Sitting across from Boone, I realized I couldn't remember the last time I'd had a conversation with someone who wasn't Dad or Pauly, or one that didn't involve logistics, like discussing microphone placement with a stagehand. Not that my conversations with Dad involved much more than logistics.

Maybe that's why I'd let a sexist cowboy drive me to a truck stop. I was starved for conversation. I lowered my menu, looking at the guy across from me. He was studying his own menu with a look of concentration too intense for hash browns and patty melts, his bottom lip caught between his teeth as he read.

"So, Boone Wyant," I asked, "are you really from Nashville, or are you from Nashville like a pre–pop music Taylor Swift was from Nashville?"

He grinned, laughing at my slight Swifty shade.

"Born and raised in the Volunteer State. Ever heard of a place called the Heartless Café?"

"Can't say that I have."

"Ouch, that one hurts." He placed his hands over his heart like I'd stabbed him with my not-very-clean butter knife.

"Sorry." I shrugged. "Is that a restaurant? Or a music venue? Country music isn't really my thing."

"This isn't just about country music, girl. This is about something that might be even more important." He lowered his menu and leaned toward me conspiratorially. "This is about *biscuits*."

I laughed in spite of myself.

"Nobody thinks biscuits are that important."

"That's how I know *you're* not from Tennessee." He shook his finger at me. "We have a very strict policy of forced exile for all biscuit haters."

"I'm not a biscuit *hater*!" I protested. "I just don't think there's anything that's more important than music."

"I can tell," he said. "I'm sure anyone who's heard you sing would say the same thing."

We locked eyes, and I found my cheeks warming under the intensity of his gaze. He was looking at me like he *knew* me, which was impossible. We hadn't even been at this table together long enough to get glasses of water.

"So. The Heartless Café?" I prompted, flustered by the charged moment we'd shared.

"Right, right." He leaned back against his booth, the tension broken. "My great-grandma opened the place in the '30s. It's right off the highway in Nashville, before you get to downtown. It's a restaurant, with fried chicken and fifteen different kinds of pie and the best biscuits you've ever tasted. And every Friday and Saturday night, there's live country music. Some of the biggest names in country have played there. Johnny Cash. Dolly Parton. Loretta Lynn. Luke Bryan and Kacey Musgraves both came through this summer."

"And let me guess—little baby Boone Wyant got his start singing at his great-grandma's knee?" I asked.

"Pretty much." The boy had a gold-record smile, and it was twisting up my insides and making me weak at the knees in ways I didn't want to acknowledge. "When she passed, my grandma took over the business, then when *she* retired a couple years ago, she passed the torch to my parents. I've been in that restaurant my whole life. Doing my homework with a basket of biscuits in front of me. Learning to play guitar. Singing in the restaurant before the real stars showed up."

"And now you're on your way to being a real star."

"Something like that," he said. "I play some jazz guitar, too, but I mostly write and sing country songs. Hoping to be the next Sam Hunt. Although, right now, it doesn't feel like that. The Stranahan is the biggest gig I've got planned by a mile. I've even had trouble filling in the rest of my tour—way too many quiet nights for my liking." He shook his head, like he was trying to clear it, and then changed the subject, charming smile firmly fixed in its usual place. "What about you, Josie McCoy? You gonna travel the world singing jazz with your old man forever?"

"Hardly." I was having a better time than I expected with Dad, but this wasn't it for me. I didn't want to be anybody's backup. "I'm gonna be a solo artist. The next Diana Ross."

"I can see it." He nodded. "Y'all been on the road for a long time? You like it?"

"Sometimes." I placed my menu down, choosing my words carefully. "I realized that you're the first person I've really talked to since we left. And I don't miss my hometown, exactly—it's kind of a complicated place—but I miss—"

"Belonging," Boone supplied. "Having some place to go home to." I nodded along with him. That was it, exactly. "It's hard being out on the road. Easy to feel like you're not tied to anything. Although, there's something to be said for that, too. That sense of freedom."

"I guess." I looked around. *Is our waitress ever coming over?* "I can definitely see myself settling somewhere, but it would have to be a really special city. Some place I could become a star."

"Nashville," he said automatically. "You have to come to Nashville. It's the best city in the world to launch a career. So many legends have gotten their start there."

"How many Black female vocalists do you know who came out of Nashville?" I asked skeptically.

Before he could admit that the country music scene was whiter than winter at the North Pole, my phone rang. I glanced at the screen, and my heart sank. Dad.

Sighing, I picked it up, and answered cautiously.

"Hey, Dad."

"Josie." He sounded *pissed*. I winced at the tone in his voice. "Where, exactly, are you?"

It was time to face the music—but not the good kind.

CHAPTER THIRTEEN
Katy

I TOOK A STEP BACK, looking at the jumpsuit on my dress form. It was sleeveless, with a high neckline, a slim waistband, and a ruffle running down the right side, all done in fuchsia crepe. I'd scrapped the original dress I'd shown Jorge, then started piecing this together. After almost a full twenty-four hours of nonstop work, I technically had a finished look, but it still wasn't feeling right.

What was wrong with it? Mom would know. I squeezed my eyes tight, imagining her by my side, assessing my jumpsuit with her cool gaze, hand poised over the pincushion on her wrist. With a tuck here or a tweak there, she'd make it perfect. Why couldn't I do the same?

Is it the ruffle? Maybe it was the ruffle. I rummaged around in my sewing kit until I found my seam ripper, then carefully started removing the ruffle without damaging the bodice underneath, trying not to mourn the hours I'd spent meticulously pleating the slippery fabric.

And without the ruffle it looked . . . boring. Totally generic. Exactly what I *didn't* want. I should probably just start over, which meant I had exactly nothing to show for the past couple days of work, and the first fitting was less than a week away.

My phone dinged with a calendar notification. Distracted, I reached over to silence it . . . then saw the alert that KO's boxing match was starting in an hour. *KO's boxing match is starting in an hour?!* That was *barely* enough time to get to Queens, and I definitely couldn't leave the house in my pink heart-printed bathrobe.

And the shirt! I had to find my lucky shirt!! The first time I went to one of KO's boxing matches, I made myself a white T-shirt that said "I <3 KO" on the front. That day, KO had done phenomenally well, and the shirt had become a bit of a lucky charm. KO wasn't as superstitious as some of the boxers I'd met, but he had his things. On match days, he always had a bowl of Lucky Charms for breakfast (hard to get more literal than that), he always wore athletic socks with red toes, and I was always front-row center, wearing my "I <3 KO" shirt. It had gotten a little short over the last couple years of washing and drying, but that just meant it worked really well with my high-waisted red palazzo pants.

Which meant I also had to find the pants!

Eventually, I found the pants hanging over the back of a chair (why?!) and the shirt in a basket of clean laundry I'd meant to put away but never folded. After dressing like I was trying to set a new speed record, I shoved a handful of accessories, some makeup, and my hairbrush into my "Sew Much Fabric Sew Little Time" tote bag. It wasn't the first time I'd finished pulling my look together on the subway, and I knew it wouldn't be the last. After a moment's hesitation, I tossed my sketchbook in there, too. Maybe something would come to me when I least expected it.

Someone must have been watching out for me, because I miraculously made it to the boxing gym before the match started. It was warm in there, the seats around the ring already mostly filled, and it smelled like sweat. I opened my phone camera to see what the insane crush on the N train had done to my hair. Miraculously, it was still mostly in place, tied back with the silk scarf Jorge had given me for my birthday last year. He'd presented it to me with the caveat that he'd found it in a bin at Larry's Vintage in the Village and it was probably a knockoff and not really Hermès, but I didn't care. It had a red-and-blue print of the Battery in Lower Manhattan, and I loved it. With a final twist to set Mom's old gold hoop earrings into place, you couldn't even tell that I'd spent the last hour crushed under someone's armpit on the subway.

Looking around the room for KO, a pair of sapphire-blue silky boxing shorts caught my eye. You know, they had kind of an interesting silhouette. I pulled my sketchbook out of my tote bag. Inspiration really could strike in the most unlikely places! Maybe a silk culotte with a wide, high, gathered waistband? Part of a two-piece set, with a cropped, off-the-shoulder top? Or maybe something more structured? Or athleisure-inspired? *No, that isn't it.* I erased the hastily drawn shoulders at the top of my sketch. It wasn't quite right.

Nothing was.

"Katy!" I looked up and spotted KO's head in the group of people milling around the ring, towering above everyone around him. He waved and made his way toward me, his broad shoulders easily carving his way through the crowd. KO was already wearing his silky red boxing shorts, but he still had a sweatshirt on. "Thank you so much for coming." He wrapped me up into a hug. I could practically feel the pre-match adrenaline coursing through him. He was never nervous, exactly, but there was always a different energy about him right before a match. "It means so much to me to have you here. And I know how busy you are with the fashion show coming up—"

"Hey, I've never missed a match before. I'm not about to start now." And honestly, I could use a break from thinking about Rex London. I wasn't about to unload all this on KO right before a fight—he needed all his focus to make sure he wasn't, you know, beaten to a pulp—but panic was definitely starting to set in. I'd never been stuck like this before.

"Well, it means a lot that my fashion mogul could take time away from her design empire to come out here for the match." He kissed the top of my head. I loved it when he did that.

"Yeah, that's me, the fashion mogul." I smiled at him, trying to project a confidence I didn't feel. "The fashion mogul and the boxing champ: New York's hottest power couple."

"Let's hope so." KO kissed his fingers and tapped the shoulder of my T-shirt three times, another thing he did for good luck. "I've got a good feeling about this match tonight. I was supposed to fight some kid from Riverdale—"

"Riverdale? Seriously? Like the Riverdale Veronica moved to?" What a weird coincidence.

"I guess so." KO shrugged. "But the guy pulled out of the match. He had some crazy excuse—I don't know how your friend Veronica's been there for so long; this Riverdale place sounds *nuts*. But anyway, Ronkowski stepped in at the last minute. He's been winning a lot, but Coach says I've never looked better . . ."

A pair of distinctly female arms appeared around KO's torso and squeezed. *Huh?* I took a step back, wobbling on my wedges, literally taken aback.

"You ready, champ?" An absolutely adorable blonde popped her head out around KO's side, her arms still tight around his middle.

"Jinx!" KO exclaimed with delight. He wrapped his

arm around her head like he was putting her in a headlock, but, you know, like a fun, hugging kind.

"Jinx?" I repeated, wondering if I'd heard him wrong. *This* was Jinx, KO's favorite new boxer at the gym?! KO released her from the headlock and she stood at his side, one arm still around his waist. She was short, about my height, and fit perfectly under KO's arm—just like I always did. Jinx's blonde hair was in two tight French braids. She wore a black sports bra and a pair of low-rise, oversize sweatpants, exposing a toned, tanned midsection. I tried to count her abs and gave up once I realized she had *more* than a six-pack.

Jinx was . . . not what I expected.

And why was she *hugging* KO? Why was she *still* hugging him? Like, a quick hug hello, I totally got, but she *still* had her arm wrapped around him. What was up with that?! I knew boxing was a physical sport, but I thought it was more, you know, punching. Less embracing. Less standing so comfortably, so casually, snuggled up under my boyfriend's arm. If anyone happened to be walking by right now, they'd think the two of them were dating! Honestly, right now, they looked like two extremely buff, sweaty people posing for a prom photo.

Just like KO *and I* had done only a couple months ago.

"Katy Keene," KO introduced us, interrupting my spiraling train of thought, "meet Julie 'Jinx' Holliday, the undefeated flyweight terror of Queens."

"This is Katy?!" Jinx pulled me into a hug that felt more

like a headlock. "KO, you weren't kidding. She's absolutely gorgeous. Love those earrings. I wish I could wear hoops in the ring, but that's kind of a professional liability."

"Sounds like a good way to lose an earlobe," I said, patting her awkwardly on the back.

I felt silly for assuming Jinx was a guy, but I had. And not that it really mattered—of course KO could have female friends—but I just hadn't expected the person KO was spending all of his time with to be so . . . well, female. And pretty.

And clearly so comfortable touching KO.

"Can you believe this guy?!" Jinx threw her arms around KO again, squeezing his middle. And again with the hugging. My fingers itched to pry her arms away so I could hug KO myself. Who *was* I right now? Some bodega cat marking my territory? *Get it together, Keene.* "He's the greatest—inside the ring and out of it." Outside the ring? How much time had they been spending together outside the ring? I tried to remember how many times KO had told me he'd grabbed a meal with Jinx after training, but back when I'd thought she was a boxer bro, I hadn't been paying enough attention. "Ronkowski's not gonna know what hit him tonight!" Jinx turned to KO. "Did you see him taping his right hand? Heard he's got a weak cross. Always has, and one of the guys told me he's been leaving that whole side unprotected recently."

"A weak cross?" KO asked. "Huh. What's wrong with it?"

"Spins his back foot," Jinx said. "Really reduces the drive."

"Really." KO nodded, rubbing his jaw.

"Mmm, yeah, a spin," I said. "Totally reducing."

Why was I jumping in here? I didn't know anything about boxing. I came to all of KO's matches, but I knew as much about it as he knew about fashion: practically nothing. And I'd never thought that was a problem before. But now, hearing him talk to Jinx about the thing he loved most in the world, I found myself feeling jealous that I couldn't share this with him the way Jinx could. It was like they were connecting in a way that KO and I never had.

"For sure," Jinx agreed with me. If she had any clue that I had no idea what I was talking about, she didn't show it. "And he telegraphs the punch. Tries to hit too hard—probably because he's compensating for the spin."

"You hate to see a telegraph," I said. Why was I *still* pretending I knew anything about a weak cross?

"Is it the drawback?" KO asked. "That's the tell?"

"Bingo," Jinx confirmed. "You'll have him knocked out in no time. That's why they call you KO. Right, Katy?" Jinx's smile was warm and open as she leaned her head against KO, tucked up so cozily under his arm.

"Right!" I smiled, and then laughed, too loudly. Jinx joined in, laughing delightedly, and so did KO, who mostly looked confused.

"Well, I should probably finish warming up," KO said. "Katy, I reserved a seat in the front for you, right next to

Mom. You can't miss her. She's wearing a sweatshirt with my face on it." He rolled his eyes, but I knew how much he loved his mom's support, face-sweatshirts and all.

"And I'm sitting on your other side!" Jinx cheered. "Let me just grab my jacket, and then I'll come find you."

"Actually, Jinx, can you help me stretch out my traps first?" KO asked, placing a hand on his shoulder as he rolled it back a few times.

"Oh my god, of course. Are they bothering you again?" She scooted behind him and placed her small hands on his shoulders, massaging them deeply.

"Ooh yeah, Jinx, that's perfect." KO closed his eyes and lowered his head. "That's the spot right there."

"Well . . . great, then!" An awkward smile was frozen on my face. "Definitely gotta . . . gotta get those traps! And I'll just, uh, go . . . over here . . ."

As I awkwardly side-shuffled away from them, they didn't appear to even notice I was gone, lost in their massage reverie.

Massaging was probably a totally normal part of boxing. And stretching a trap definitely seemed really important. And it's not like I could do this for KO. I didn't know how to massage a trap. I wasn't even sure where his trap was! But watching Jinx touch KO had woken up some weird, jealous girl part of me that I didn't recognize, and I definitely didn't like.

The slice of ninety-nine-cent pizza I'd eaten on my run to the train churned uncomfortably in my stomach.

I bobbed and weaved my way through the crowd until I found my seat next to Mrs. Kelly.

"Katy!" She pulled me into a hug, squashing my face against the KO face screen-printed on her white sweatshirt. "How's our boy looking?"

"Great," I said. "He looks great."

And he did. Even with the excited pre-match chatter, I could pick KO's laugh out of the crowd. I followed the sound and found him at the side of the ring, Jinx wrapping his hands as he got ready to put on his boxing gloves. They were both laughing over some shared joke, KO more relaxed and confident than I'd ever seen him before a match, and he looked down at her like . . .

Well, like he looked at me.

CHAPTER FOURTEEN
Jorge

THE MORNING AFTER THE DANCE call, I shimmied around the back room of the bodega as I took inventory. I must have heard "Put On Your Sunday Clothes" about fifty times last night, but I still couldn't stop listening to it. This bish may not have had a parasol, but my world was all a smile, baby.

Something tapped me on the shoulder. I practically jumped out of my skin as I turned to confront my assailant.

"Ma!" I shouted. She winced at the noise. I took off my headphones to yell at her at a normal volume. "Don't sneak up on me like that!"

"Sorry, sorry, m'hijo." She held up her hands in apology. "So? How did it go?"

She waited in front of me expectantly. In the tiny stockroom, there was barely room for both of us. I leaned back against the paper towels, trying to get a little space.

"How did what go? Reading that amazing issue of *People* you left me?" I asked innocently.

"Very funny. I saw you leave the house with your lucky green audition shorts last night. Does that mean you made it through to the dance call?"

"Do you realize how messed up this is?" I faced her with my hands on my hips. "You leave me secret audition notices like we're in some kind of Nancy Drew mystery, you follow me into the stockroom while I'm doing inventory to ask how it went . . . Is this all just 'cuz you don't want to talk to me when Dad is around?"

"Your dad is still having a hard time accepting your . . . lifestyle."

"He's had literal *years* to get used to the idea. And I hate that phrase." I rolled my eyes. "'Lifestyle' makes being gay sound like being into cats. Or macramé. Like it's a choice."

"I'm sorry. I didn't know that. I'm learning, okay?" Ma said earnestly. "Will you tell me about the dance call? It's so important to audition well. You know, when I was a Rockette, we had to audition at the open call every year, even if we'd been in the show before."

"Yeah, Ma, I know." Ma and I had always been able to bond about our love of dance. She'd taught me my first-ever kick-and-turn combo. I was barely walking, but I had the best turnout in the history of toddlers.

"So? Did my baby kill it?" she asked.

"What do you think?" Even though we were still in a weird place, I couldn't stop myself from sharing with her how proud I was. Ma would have been *living* for how I slayed last night. She always lost her mind at curtain call for my shows in high school, screaming louder than everybody else's parents combined. "Obviously he killed it."

I *always* killed it at dance calls, and last night was no exception. The dance call had been held in another big black box space, the same bald man sitting at another black piano. There must have been at least thirty of us there, with even more milling about in the hallway, either waiting to go in or lingering after finishing up with the previous group. After checking in with the monitor, I safety-pinned the number she gave me to my crop top, and rolled my lucky green audition shorts up one more time for good measure.

When you've got legs like these, you don't hide 'em away behind dance pants.

I took a spot front-row center, because, hello, they weren't giving out trophies for being shy. If Ethan Fox wanted to see me, then he was going to *see me*. The choreographer broke down the combo, and from the first time through, I knew I had this in the bag. When God handed out gifts, she didn't just give me a cute butt and a gorgeous face, she also gave me a freaky-good ability to remember choreography.

Strong arms pop up, melt down, collapse the body, legs open and close, kick, kick, point, put on the fake bowler hat, turn, chest roll, fan kick, *pose!*

If I had enough space, I could turn out the whole thing perfectly right here, right now.

I'd stayed front-row center for every run-through, even as they started cutting people. But not me. By the end of the night, they'd only invited four of us in my group to callbacks on Monday, where we'd actually read some lines from the script. There was still a long way to go, but I'd already gotten past so many other people. This could really happen. *Me*, a working actor on Broadway. The thing I'd wanted for my whole life.

Just call me the Man of La Mancha, because it wasn't such an impossible dream.

Mom squealed and pulled me into a hug, bringing me back to the present. It had been so long since I'd been close enough to her to smell her perfume, and the faint whiff of grease that clung to her from spending too much time near the flat top in the bodega. I started to pull away, but she clutched me tighter.

Too tightly.

I wasn't ready to have our big family reconciliation moment in a room the size of a closet stuffed with paper goods and nonperishable food items.

I knew I had to forgive my parents; not because they deserved it, but for my own mental health. I couldn't keep carrying around the burden of all my bad feelings about them. But forgiveness was a lot easier in theory than in practice.

When my parents had kicked me out, I'd been in such shock, I could barely even process it. Instead of dealing with my feelings, I ignored them. I felt safe cuddling up with Katy, singing show tunes and bedazzling sweatshirts. The only thing I wanted to feel was that safety, not the hurt from what my family had done. Later, when my parents had come downtown to Katy's to invite me back home, I'd been angry, but also pathetically grateful that they wanted me back—that they were trying, at least a little bit.

But Mom and Dad's trying had begun and ended with asking me to come home. We'd been living together like this for *years*, tiptoeing around all the things we didn't want to talk about. My parents had still never apologized. And I'd been pushing my pain down, down, down, until I almost couldn't feel it anymore, because I had to. It was the only way I could survive. But I was tired of pretending that waiting for a "sorry" that was never going to come wasn't killing me slowly, one piece at a time.

"I miss you," she said quietly. "I miss *us*. I miss the way things were, before all this."

"I miss you, too." That much, at least, was true. "But being gay isn't an 'all this,' Ma. It's just me. Who I am. So there's no going back to the way things were. There's only forward. We have to figure out a new way to be."

"I'd really like to. Figure out a new way." Ma leaned back and looked up at me. It was what I wanted, too. But if Dad kept treating me like a ghost, and Ma wouldn't talk to me in front of him, it would be hard to figure anything out.

"So? The dance call?" She squeezed my arms.

"I really did kill it," I said, smiling. Broadway was always safe territory. Maybe this was how we would find a new way forward, by talking about my career. "I'm moving on to the next round of callbacks on Monday."

"Of course you are, m'hijo. Because you got it from your mama." She pinched my cheek.

I had gotten so much from her. My sense of rhythm. My love of the spotlight. My understanding of the importance of accessorizing.

But if I couldn't share *all* of who I was with her, then did any of that even matter?

"Hey, Ma!" Joaquin, one of my older brothers, popped his head into the stockroom. "What's up, little bro?"

"Baby!" Ma exclaimed with delight. Now that they'd all moved out, anytime one of them came home, Ma practically busted out the confetti. "What are you doing here?"

"I brought you something." Joaquin leaned down to kiss her on the cheek. "Chef sent me home with some rib eye."

"Are you walking around with raw meat in your bag?" I asked.

"I wrapped it up!" He pulled out a ziplock bag with a very rare, bloody steak. "Unfortunately, this is the closest I've gotten to any protein," he said sadly. "It's still nothing but washing produce. I've scrubbed so many beets my fingers are permanently stained."

"Prep cook today, executive chef tomorrow." Ma

patted him on the cheek. "Look at my boys, the chef and the Broadway star."

"Chef must like you if he sent you home with that steak," I said. "Everyone knows meat is the sign of true love."

"Shut it." Joaquin pushed me into the paper towels. It was a playful shove, but like all my brothers, he was so much bulkier than me I fell right over.

"No pushing, chicos," Ma scolded. "Well? Should we go have dinner? Maybe I'll call the rest of your brothers."

"It's not that much steak, Ma," I joked.

"Still. It would be nice. To eat as a family," Ma said hopefully.

As a family.

Maybe tonight, it would feel a little more like that.

CHAPTER FIFTEEN
Pepper

SOME PEOPLE MIGHT HAVE SAID fall in New York was too cold for swimming, but one assumed those people didn't have SoHo House memberships.

I held my breath and dove under the water, admiring my newly lavender nails as I executed a neat breaststroke. Bless whoever decided to keep this rooftop pool heated and open year-round, because this was absolutely divine. I suppose I could have taken Leo up on his invitation to join him at the Malibu house, but honestly, what would I do in Malibu? There was nowhere like New York. The energy of this city was practically addictive.

I rested my elbows on the edge of the pool, looking past the plush striped lounge chairs to the rooftops spread out before me. How should I make my perfectly Pepper mark on the city? Although I was certainly enjoying a literal float at the moment, I wasn't one to metaphorically float through life. Many people moved to New York in the hope the city would change them.

I came to New York in order to change the city.

If I really thought about it, I supposed I was itching for a room of one's own, as it were. I could have written for the *New Yorker*, like dear Jia, or done a TED Talk, like darling Brené, and perhaps I would do *both* of those things, but that couldn't be *all* I did. After doing that awful Chloe's hideous podcast interview, I couldn't stop thinking about the idea of having my very own platform, instead of simply expressing myself through another's. If Chloe "Please Buy This Tomato Leaf Candle" van Sant had enough people interested in what she had to say, surely my audience would number in the thousands.

Not that I had any interest in a podcast. Good lord, no. Any fool with an iPhone and an NPR tote bag could have a podcast. When one thought of Pepper Smith, one thought of exclusivity, and that was exactly how I intended things to remain.

"Your grapefruit matcha spritzer, Miss Smith."

The waiter deposited my drink at the side of the pool, the pretty pink color fizzing invitingly in the glass.

"Thank you so much, Pablo darling." I smiled at him. "Grapefruit is very hydrating, you know. When I was in the Hamptons last summer, Gwyneth told me it was absolutely essential to remain hydrated while submerged in chlorine. It can completely strip your hair and skin of its natural oils. Do keep that in mind, Pablo."

"I will, Miss Smith." Goodness, he really had a very nice smile. I took a sip of my drink through its black paper straw, contemplating just how handsome he was. Probably a poor idea to get romantically involved with someone at SoHo House, but the idea was tempting.

I was in New York to focus on my career, but the idea of a bit of romance wasn't entirely distasteful. I was an excellent multitasker, after all. Perhaps I should invite that gorgeous blonde from the park out to dinner . . .

"Pablo, darling," I called as he turned back to the bar with his tray. "Would you mind awfully taking a picture for me?"

"Of course not, Miss Smith. Earlier this morning I took . . . well, quite a few pictures for Miss Cabot. I believe I have a better grasp of angles now."

From everything I'd heard about her, Alexandra Cabot *would* be terribly demanding about photo angles. Resolving not to pester Pablo too much—if I needed a *true* fashion shot, I could always call Mario—I pointed to my phone on the lounge chair, and he grabbed it as I arranged myself on the edge of the pool, a darling pair of tortoiseshell cat's-eye sunglasses perched on my nose. As Pablo snapped away, I posed, making sure to show off the lovely one-shoulder neckline of my swimsuit to its best advantage.

Pablo handed me the phone to examine the pictures, and I smiled.

Even without a filter, they were perfect.

CHAPTER SIXTEEN
Josie

"SO YOU THOUGHT IT WAS a good idea to get in a car with a stranger. In the middle of the night," Dad said. He wouldn't even look at me. Dad sat in the passenger seat of our tour van, the back of his head radiating annoyance. After the epic lecture he gave me last night, I would have thought he'd have tired himself out by now, but apparently not.

Dad had been waiting for me in the lobby when I got back. The poor front desk clerk got to hear almost an hour of "What were you thinking?" and "Do I need to tape your door shut to keep you from sneaking out?"

Technically, I didn't sneak out. I just left.

It was a distinction Dad had definitely not appreciated.

Pauly turned the volume on the radio up ever so slightly, the sounds of Steely Dan filling the van. He was probably tired of the soundtrack of Dad chastising me, which had been playing on repeat throughout our drive to Cleveland.

Me too, Pauly. Me too.

"It wasn't a car," I replied. "It was a pickup truck."

"Don't be smart, Josie. Actually, *be* smart. I expected you to be *much* smarter than that." I crossed my arms against the seat belt and slumped backward, feeling all of about five years old. "What happened to 'I'm from Riverdale, I can handle myself'? You know how people don't get murdered? From Riverdale or anywhere else? They don't go to truck stops with strange boys, no matter how cute they are."

"He's not that cute," I muttered.

Lies. He *was* that cute. Dangerously cute. So cute that I had kind of forgotten about stranger danger in my need for human conversation and chocolate chip pancakes.

"I just don't know what you were thinking."

I wasn't thinking. That was the problem.

That, and a smile I still couldn't forget, even several hours into this unpleasant lecture.

"I don't know, I just . . . I felt like I knew him. I told you he was playing the same venue after us."

"Doesn't mean you know him," Dad snorted.

"And he's a fan of yours, Dad."

"I don't care about that! I'm sure I have plenty of fans who are murderers! Well, maybe not *plenty*," he amended. "But some. I'm sure I have some. Excellent taste in music doesn't mean you can't be a murderer."

"Pauly, can we pull off at the next rest stop?" I asked. "I could use a break."

"Oh, excellent, Pauly, yes, let's pull off at the rest stop," Dad said. "Who knows what kind of poor decisions Josie could make at a rest stop on the side of the highway? Maybe there's an unmarked van she could hop into!"

"Dad, I'm sorry, okay?" I snapped. Luckily, Pauly put on his blinker for the next exit, because I really did have to pee. "You're right. I shouldn't have gotten in the car of somebody I don't know. From now on, it's early bedtimes and no human contact, okay?"

"You can have human contact between the hours of eight a.m. and ten p.m.," Dad said. "With the people in this van."

"Very magnanimous, Dad, thank you."

"It is indeed magnanimous. Pauly's an excellent conversationalist," Dad said as we pulled into the parking lot.

"What do you know about bees, Josie?" Pauly asked as he parked neatly between two Priuses.

"Not much, Pauly."

"Did you know that the average bee only makes one-twelfth of a teaspoon of honey in its lifetime?"

"I did not." I unbuckled my seat belt and slid out of the van, happy to get some space from Dad's unending guilt trip. The fact was, in the slightly gray Ohio light of day, Dad made some excellent points. It *had* been pretty stupid to get in a car with someone I had just met. Usually, I considered myself to be way savvier than that. I mean, there was a reason I'd only found myself face-to-face with the Black Hood in my nightmares. Unlike the rest of the population of Riverdale, I don't actively seek out serial killers.

Well, it didn't matter now. I had no plans of seeing Boone Wyant again and no way to contact him, even if I wanted to.

"Plenty more bee facts where those came from!" Pauly called cheerfully as I walked into the rest stop.

"Oh, goody," I said under my breath as I waved half-heartedly at him. No offense to bees, or to Pauly, but discussing honey output with a middle-aged man with a ponytail for the indeterminate future was kind of a depressing prospect.

Washing my hands in the sink at the rest stop, I took a deep breath and leaned forward to look at myself in the mirror. I looked tired, the hollows under my eyes more pronounced. Maybe Dad was right, and one late bedtime really had taken a toll.

Well, I couldn't hide in here forever. The sooner we got to Cleveland, the sooner I could escape the Van of Shame. Time to hit the road and get it over with.

Dad was waiting for me at the rest stop exit. My reprieve was even shorter than I'd thought.

"You know, Josie," he said as we walked to the parking lot, "when I asked you to come on this tour, it was because I thought you were mature enough to handle it. Not just mature as a performer—and I must say, I've been impressed by the caliber of what you've brought to the stage, night after night—but mature as a *person*."

"I know, Dad."

"If it turns out you're not as mature as I'd thought . . . I have no problems sending you back home to Riverdale. None whatsoever." I hugged my leather jacket closer, feeling a chill pass over me. "I've been doing the Myles McCoy show solo for a long, long time, little girl, and I have no problem doing it solo again."

"Understood, Dad." I paused at the van door, my hand on the handle, as Dad loomed over me, glowering.

"Pull another stunt like that, and you're off the tour. Am I clear?"

"Crystal." I gritted my teeth.

Going back to Riverdale wasn't an option. I wouldn't leave the tour on anything less than my own terms, and derailing my career for a guy was not how Josie McCoy operated.

Boone Wyant wasn't a mistake I'd make again.

CHAPTER SEVENTEEN
Katy

"HI THERE," I SAID, CRADLING the phone against my neck as I knelt down to snip a loose thread off the hem of my dress, "my name is Katy Keene. I'm calling about your post for an 'exciting career in fashion'?"

I'd been scoping for job postings during sewing breaks, and nothing even *remotely* related to the fashion industry had popped up. Wasn't there someone who needed sweaters folded somewhere? I was about two minutes away from walking down to any boutique in SoHo to show them the kind of magic I could work with a steamer and beg them to take me on.

So when I'd seen a GregsList post for an "exciting career in fashion" I immediately called the listed number, despite an uninspiring vagueness about what, exactly, the job entailed.

"Great, great. Are you under five eight?" the voice on the other end of the phone asked.

"Um . . . yes?" That could not have been a good sign. Pretty sure most reputable jobs didn't have a height requirement. Unless it was roller coaster tester, and that definitely didn't constitute a career in fashion. "May I ask why that matters?"

"You gotta be under five eight to fit in the costume."

"Costume?" I repeated. Definitely a bad sign.

"Yeah, yeah, costume." The man sighed, bored. "It's a Howie the Hoagie costume. Fifteen bucks an hour to hand out flyers for Howie's Hoagies."

The job was dressing up as a sandwich. Unbelievable.

"And this is 'a career in fashion' how, exactly?"

"You'd be a model, sweetheart. Modeling the finest in sandwich couture." He cackled unkindly. "Look, you interested? I can see you at the Penn Station Howie's Hoagies tomorrow afternoon for an interview. Let's say three p.m.?"

"I'll have to, um, think about it."

"Don't think too hard. I've got interviews all day today."

He hung up on me. Sighing, I set down the phone. Was "sandwich" the only thing I was qualified for? This was the first job I'd reached out to that had even offered me an interview. I had no food service experience, and no job experience at all aside from working in my mom's shop, which looked pretty paltry on my résumé.

How does anyone in this city get a job? I texted Jorge.

Nepotism, he texted back immediately. *Want me to ask Ma if you can pick up a shift or two at the bodega?*

That's okay, I responded. It was nice of Jorge to offer, but I knew things were still weird between him and his parents. I didn't want him to ask them for a favor on my behalf. *Don't worry about it. I'm sure something will turn up.*

Just focus on turning out that dress! Jorge texted, followed by a string of unicorn emojis.

The dress. Right. I looked up at it. Technically, I *did* have a completed dress. It was a much more formal look than I'd initially intended to make. I'd hand dyed it in ombré shades of blue and created flower details along the halter neckline and belt. I was relieved to see that it actually looked pretty good.

It also looked . . . familiar . . .

Wait a minute. Did I just make Constance Wu's Marchesa dress from *Crazy Rich Asians*?

Oh my god. A quick Google search confirmed that was *exactly* what I'd done. What was wrong with me?! I'd stayed up all night working on it, and my tired subconscious must have pushed me toward something it recognized.

I'd have to go back to square one. Again. The first fitting was in two days. This was an absolute nightmare. This never would have happened if Mom was here. She would have recognized it immediately just from the sketch, and we would have laughed about it, and I wouldn't have wasted all this time I desperately needed. I bundled up the floaty hem of the dress and screamed into it, venting my frustration until Mrs. Rajput next door banged on the wall to get me to shut up.

I needed a break. I knew I should keep working, but I had to get out of this room. I picked up my phone, hoping to text my way to escape.

Want to get out of the city in a couple hours? I texted KO. *You + me + apple picking? I'll bring the cider.*

Before I could even pick up my scissors again, the phone buzzed with his reply. *Sounds great, but can we go another time? Jinx has a match tonight and I promised I'd help her warm up before.*

I stared at my phone, frowning. Obviously, I *could* go to an apple orchard by myself, but I didn't really want to. I wanted to go with KO. But he was busy with Jinx. Again.

After KO won his last match against Ronkowski, Jinx had joined us at the Starlite. She slid into the booth right after KO, leaving me stranded on the other side, all by myself.

They had looked awfully cozy in that booth.

I hadn't been able to tear my eyes away from the way she casually ate fries off his plate, like they'd been eating together forever. (Which they kind of had.) And I couldn't stop thinking about all the times KO had stayed out late, hanging with Jinx at the Starlite.

Ugh. I knew this wasn't a good look for me. Which is probably why I hadn't told Jorge about Jinx Holliday, if I was being honest. Jinx had been nothing but nice to me, and I didn't want to be the girl who didn't let her boyfriend have female friends. That was regressive and stupid, and I *knew that*.

So why was I feeling all jealous and snappy, thinking about Jinx eating KO's fries?

Before I could reply, my phone buzzed again.

Of course if it's really important to do apples today I can. No problem. Just let me know.

He was too sweet. Which only made me feel worse. KO had proven time and again that I was his priority, and I needed to give him the same respect.

Don't worry about it, I texted, followed by a heart emoji. *We can apple pick another time. Tell Jinx good luck!*

And I'd struck out again. Well, more time for me to work on the dress, I guess. Sighing, I started to painstakingly take it off the dress form, wondering if there was anything salvageable here.

This fashion show at Lacy's was a dream opportunity. I should have been *bursting* with ideas, excited to show what I could do.

So why did I feel so stuck?

I knew why. I didn't know how to sew without Mom. I didn't *want* to sew without her. But there was nothing I could do about that.

A single tear fell onto the silk, staining it a darker shade of blue.

CHAPTER EIGHTEEN
Jorge

I COULDN'T BELIEVE IT. THE clean-cut Ken doll from the open call was sitting next to the only open folding chair at my next callback. I hadn't seen him at the dance call, but they'd probably run multiple days, so that wasn't totally surprising.

Smiling as I took the seat next to him, he smiled back, a glint of something flirtatious in his eyes. *Ooh, Jorge,* I cautioned myself. *You're not here to make friends.* Or more than friends. It was time to *focus,* and I didn't mean on the hottie whose leg kept maybe-accidentally-maybe-not brushing up against mine. But as I continued sneaking peeks at the all-American angel sitting next to me, he was looking more and more kissable.

"Keller?" the audition monitor called. "Kevin Keller?"

"That's me." So the hottie's name was Kevin Keller. Totally basic, but this boy was *working* basic and turning it into an art form. He smoothed a hand over his chestnut hair and stood up. Mmm, I'd forgotten how tall he was.

"Break a leg in there." I couldn't resist saying something to him. I should have been doing vocal warm-ups or something, but instead, I was trying to smolder at some guy in a *polo shirt*. Who was I right now?

"Thanks." He smiled, and I swear a little twinkle shot out of his smile, like he was in a toothpaste commercial. "You too."

Okay, now it was time to really get serious. I pulled my highlighted sides out of my dance bag and smoothed them. I'd been going over my lines like crazy ever since they were emailed to me, but there were only so many ways you could say "Holy cabooses!" before it felt completely surreal. I'd even called Katy to read for her, but I could tell she'd been distracted over the phone. Not that I blamed her; she had a lot of stuff going on with the fashion show, but I wished we could have hung out in person instead. That girl needed to move uptown, STAT. The Lower East Side was over, anyway. It was all UPPAbaby strollers and eighteen-dollar oat milk lattes now.

"Jorge?" I blessed the audition monitor for not pronouncing it "George," like some of my high school teachers had. "Jorge Lopez?"

"That's me." I smiled my very best "cast me" smile, even though I knew the likelihood of the casting people asking her opinion about the most castable smiles in the hallway was slim. "You're on deck."

"Great, thank you so much." I looked back at my lines. They were memorized at this point, but I couldn't keep myself from scanning the page over and over again, trying to do something, anything that would make me feel ready.

"Holy cabooses," I whispered. "Holy cabooses."

The door to the audition room opened, and Kevin Keller came through. I tried to read on his face how it had gone, but his neutral smile told me nothing.

"Jorge Lopez?" the monitor called, nodding at me. "You're up."

"Thank you." I smiled at her again, determined to be the friendliest bish in the hallway. She held the door open for me, and I walked back into the black box. There was the same panel of people behind the table, only this time, a woman with glasses and a ponytail sat slightly to the side, a binder in her lap. That must have been the reader.

"Jorge!" Ethan Fox said from the middle of the table, a warm smile on his face. *They want to like you*, I reminded myself, in Ma's voice. Ethan Fox, at least, was certainly acting like he did. "Great to see you again, man. Go ahead and get started whenever you're ready."

"Thank you." Nobody was more thankful than actors at auditions. Like, truly, had a more desperate group ever existed? I took my spot in the center of the room, made eye contact with the reader, and nodded to let her know I was ready.

"Barnaby, you and I are going to New York," she read in

a complete monotone, her eyes firmly locked on the page.

I kept my script in my hands even though I didn't need it to deliver my lines, listening and reacting like the reader was giving me something instead of the absolute nothing she was serving. Like, I knew it wasn't her job to emote, but come on. I'd seen more acting out of my brother Miguel when he helped me run lines for my role as Officer Krupke in high school, and Miguel was a chauffeur. Not exactly an artistic profession.

"And one more thing." Man, this reader was so flat, it was like acting with a post. "We're not coming back to Yonkers until we each fall in love with someone cute."

"Holy cabooses!" I exclaimed, throwing up my hands. "Cornelius, we can't do that! We don't even *know* anyone cute!"

Everyone behind the table laughed. I smiled with triumph, preparing for my next line.

"Hold on a minute, Jorge." Ethan Fox stopped. I turned away from the reader, surprised. They'd all just cracked up. What was the problem? "Just a quick note for you."

"Great." I smiled, because God help you if you weren't gagging for criticism at an audition.

"We're looking for a read that's a little less . . ." Ethan Fox paused, like he was struggling to pick the word. "A little less, hmm . . ."

"Less soft," the woman suggested.

"A little less gay," the man with the bald head and glasses said flatly.

Ex*cuse* me? I stared at the casting people, shocked that some of them were actually nodding along. This wasn't the army in the '90s. You couldn't just go around telling people to be less gay! Especially not in a *theater* of all places! The theater had always been my sacred space where I could just be *me*, no judgment, ever since I was a little gay-by. And I was willing to bet that at least half the people behind the panel felt the same way, including, perhaps, Mister Be-Less-Gay Bald Head himself.

"Maybe more of a masculine energy, is what he means." Ethan Fox gestured with his hands, like masculine energy could be conveyed in a gesture.

"There's a lot of different ways to be masculine," I shot back. "My sexuality doesn't have anything to do with my gender expression."

"Of course not," he said conciliatorily. "It's just, you know, Barnaby does have a heterosexual relationship—"

"Who says?" I knew I was being combative, and I should probably just roll over and take the criticism if I wanted the part, but I did not survive four years of high school gym class to be told I was "too gay" by some middle-aged theatre queens who probably wished they were on my side of the table, looking this killer in tight pants.

"It's in the text," the reader pointed out unhelpfully.

"Barnaby could be bi. Minnie Fay doesn't have to be a cis woman. I thought this production was going to be different from some community theatre show in Iowa. Isn't that, like, the whole point of what you do as a director? I thought that was the whole Ethan Fox thing. You do new works, or you break old works down and make them new again, in ways nobody's thought of before? Because you're such a daring experimental genius or whatever?"

Everyone behind the table exchanged looks like they couldn't believe I was talking to the director like that. I kind of couldn't believe it, either, but whatever. Even at eighteen, I was too old for that fragile straight boy nonsense.

"You know what? Let's call it for today," Ethan said.

And there goes my chance at Broadway. I'd probably feel bad about it later, but right now, I was too pissed to even think about what I was missing out on.

"But, Jorge, I'd still really like to see you at the next callback. Get you to read with some of the actors auditioning for Cornelius." The other people behind the table looked as surprised as I felt. *I'm still in this thing, even after all that?*

"Great, sure, yeah. Thank you so much."

As I waved good-bye and headed out, I wondered if I even cared that I made it to the next round of callbacks. Did I still want to be cast in this production of *Hello, Dolly!*? I wasn't sure. Any environment where I couldn't really be *me* wasn't one I wanted to be part of. But being on Broadway had been my only dream, since before I could even read sheet music. What if it was like this everywhere?

No one had ever told me I was too anything in a

theater. It was the one place where I was never too loud. Too skinny. Too *gay*. But maybe it had just been that way at school and at camp. Maybe, now that I was trying to be a real working actor, that was all over.

The idea of giving up on my dreams was awful.

But having to hide who I was to make them come true was even worse.

Cutting through my inner monologue of nonstop angst, I could hear Ma's voice in my head warning me not to burn any bridges. Better to go home now and see if I could talk it through with Katy before I made a decision, especially while I was still so angry.

"Hold on a minute, Jorge." Much to my surprise, Ethan Fox emerged from behind the table and jogged over to meet me by the door. Up close, he was even younger than I'd thought. I could see a smattering of freckles across his nose, and only a faint crease of lines by his eyes. "Listen," he said quietly. "I really like you, and I'm sorry for the way Gilbert delivered that note. It was unprofessional, and uneducated, and I am truly sorry." I would have preferred the apology accompanied by a heaping side of calling Gilbert out for being a bigot, but it was something, I guess. "I think you can bring a lot to this production. You have a great voice, you're a phenomenal dancer, you actually look seventeen, and you clearly have a knack for comedy. I'm definitely interested in seeing the Barnaby that *you* can create. Like I said, we just need an energy that's more—"

"Masculine," I finished for him. Right now, Ethan

Fox was every gym teacher I'd ever had. He was my dad not understanding why I wanted to be Princess Jasmine for Halloween as a little kid. He was my brother Hugo making fun of me for "throwing like a girl." It was hard to even look at him.

"Exactly. I mean, there's a great tradition of truly grounded, masculine dancing in the American musical theatre canon. That's what I'm trying to tap into. Think, you know, more Gene Kelly in *An American in Paris*, less Billy Porter in *Kinky Boots*."

"Mmm-hmm." Ethan Fox should be *gagging* to get Billy Porter in one of his shows. But I kept that thought to myself.

"Think about it, okay?" He reached out and squeezed my shoulder. "I know I shouldn't say this at this point in the process, but I'm rooting for you."

Ethan Fox was rooting for *me*? This situation was way more complicated than the choreography at the dance call. Even with my hurt and disappointment, part of me couldn't help but feel excited that I had a real shot at this. And *Ethan Fox*, probably the most famous director working in New York right now, was rooting for *me*, some unknown kid who'd never booked a professional gig. It was unreal.

Think about it.

I couldn't promise anything else, but that, at least, I could do.

CHAPTER NINETEEN
Pepper

"GIRL CRUSH!"
by Amelie Stafford for *CelebutanteTalk*,
a subsidiary of Cabot Media

We've got a girl crush, and it's not just on the divine Miss Pepper Smith! We should have known it wouldn't take our girl Pep long to perform a royal rebound. Last night, the perfect Pepper was spotted locking lips with an unidentified gorgeous blonde in a too-chic-for-words sequined silver jumpsuit.

Patrons at Il Boccone NYC, the hot new restaurant from up-and-coming chef Blaze Rossi, immediately spotted Pepper canoodling with her date over a plate of pappardelle.

Guess who was also in attendance? Notoriously prickly celebrity chef Gordon Ramsay.

When Gordon started complaining loudly about his improperly prepared pasta, Pepper saved the day by running to the kitchen, whipping up a quick carbonara, and serving it to the chef, who immediately pronounced it the best he'd ever eaten. Is there anything our girl can't do?! Blaze Rossi offered to make Pepper chef de cuisine on the spot, but unfortunately, she had to decline, citing other pressing engagements.

We here at *CelebutanteTalk* can't wait to hear what those pressing engagements are! Perhaps a pasta pop-up of her very own? Rumors have swirled for years that Pepper Smith hosts an extremely exclusive, secret underground supper club whenever she's in the city, frequented by the likes of Timothée Chalamet and the Hadid sisters. Perhaps it's time to open the doors so us mere mortals can dine like Pepper does!

Now, there's only one question all in-the-know New Yorkers are dying to know—who's the lucky lady who's captured the heart (or at least the lips) of the toast of the town? We've been scanning Pepper's Insta for clues, but she hasn't posted anything since her gorgeous shot from the roof-deck pool of SoHo House. (Swipe up on the latest @CelebutanteTalk Instastory to purchase the exact swimsuit Pepper Smith was wearing!) If you recognize the mystery blonde (or have any other Pepper sightings!), please send any information to Amelie.Stafford@cabotmediagroup.com.

CHAPTER TWENTY
Josie

THE FASHIONS AT THE BISCUIT Barrel were really something else. Although, I'm not sure what exactly I should have expected from a combined restaurant and country store. In addition to learning more than I ever needed to know about bees, I'd also recently discovered that Pauly had a deep and abiding love for the Biscuit Barrel's hash browns, and now I felt like we'd had breakfast in every Biscuit Barrel in Ohio and Pennsylvania.

We'd played a couple of less-than-stellar shows in Youngstown and Akron—not that there was anything wrong with the *shows*, but the venues weren't great, and the seats weren't full. Delivering a show to empty seats was a lot harder than I thought it would be. I couldn't wait to get to Pittsburgh tomorrow. No matter how many people were there, I knew someone special would be in the audience: Kevin. He must have been really busy with his first semester—I hadn't heard from him since I told him we were coming through Pittsburgh—but I couldn't wait to see him.

Assuming we ever got out of this Biscuit Barrel.

Pauly was busy trying to beat the peg game they had on every table, and Dad was trying to get the waitress to give him some kind of fancy coffee drink that I was pretty sure was out of the purview of a Biscuit Barrel barista, so who knew how long that would take. While they were otherwise occupied, I was shopping. I pulled a sweater off the rack, agog at the bright red cardinal sitting inside a snow globe that boasted real falling snow glitter. This was so hideous it was almost cool? I faced the mirror, holding the sweater up to my shoulders, wondering what Dad would do if I rolled up for our next show wearing this monstrosity instead of one of my typically chic all-black ensembles.

Behind me, a handsome, stubbled face rose over my shoulder. I watched my jaw drop in the mirror as Boone Wyant ambled closer, his hands in the pockets of his jeans. He was wearing a cozy flannel shirt over another tight Henley, and I was starting to think that between Boone and Archie, I might have some kind of undiagnosed clinical addiction to Henleys. A flirty grin broke out across his face as our reflections made eye contact.

"If anyone could pull that off, it's you, Josie McCoy."

"So you really are stalking me." I put the sweater back on the rack and turned to face him, trying to play it cool, even though I was feeling decidedly uncool. The fact that

I was wearing an old pair of River Vixens sweatpants and a plain black hoodie definitely wasn't helping matters. I always felt my best when I was dressed in something performance ready, but even I didn't see the point of riding around in a van while dressed to the nines. Now, however, I wished I was looking a little bit more like my usual fabulous self. If nothing else, the height advantage of a good pair of heels would have been nice. I tried to stand a bit taller in my favorite pair of pink-and-black Nikes, unused to the way Boone towered over me.

"Swear I'm not!" He held up his hands. "I just have an addiction to Goo Goo Clusters."

"Now you're just making up words."

"Absolutely not."

Boone moved forward, an arm outstretched. He leaned over me, so close that for a wild moment I thought he was about to kiss me. He wasn't, of course. Obviously. We didn't even know each other. And a Biscuit Barrel gift shop wasn't exactly conducive to romance.

But being that close to Boone made me feel some kind of way. He smelled like clean laundry and a little bit of leather, and I couldn't resist breathing deep.

"Got it," Boone said, grunting slightly with effort. From the shelf behind my head, he pulled out two square, blue candy wrappers. "Goo Goo Clusters," he announced. "This is the pecan flavor, my favorite. Caramel, marshmallow, pecans, chocolate, all the best things. And made right in Nashville," he added proudly.

"Do you work for the board of tourism there or something?" I rolled my eyes, but his hometown pride was kind of cute. "Is the city of Nashville sponsoring you? If I go to one of your shows, will I find 'Visit Nashville' stickers plastered all over your amp?"

"You wanna come to one of my shows?" The excitement that lit up his eyes was pretty flattering. "Any chance you'll be in Pittsburgh tomorrow night? I'm playing Lonesome Cowboy."

"Lonesome Cowboy?" I repeated, wondering what kind of venue that was.

"Yeah. It's a bar." He ducked his head a little, like he was embarrassed. "But it's a great venue. Always an awesome crowd. More country fans than you'd think in Pittsburgh. I always love the energy of a bar crowd."

"I know what you mean." I thought of how much fun it had been to sing at La Bonne Nuit. Last I'd heard, it was more dance club than speakeasy, but I'd still had some great nights there.

"So? You heading anywhere near Pittsburgh?" he prompted.

"I'm playing Pittsburgh tomorrow night. So I'll be there, but otherwise occupied."

"You might be able to come, anyway. I'm doing an eight p.m. and a late-night show, so you could come after your gig. Where are you playing?"

"Carnegie Hall."

"Fancy." He whistled.

"It's not the one in New York—"

"It's still real nice. Beautiful venue. You're gonna love it."

"Have you been there? How long have you been on the road for?" I asked curiously.

"On my own, just for the past couple months, since I turned eighteen. But when I was younger, I used to tour with my parents and brothers, before my parents took over the day-to-day operations at the Heartless Café. We had a family folk band."

"You're kidding." I snorted, imagining Boone running around in a sailor suit like a little Von Trapp.

"Hey, what's that tone? You're basically in a family band right now, missy."

"You can go ahead and add 'missy' to the list of no-no names, along with 'darlin',' 'ma'am,' please don't even think about busting out 'sweetheart' . . ." I ticked them off on my fingers.

"My bad. Apology Goo Goo?" He held one out to me.

"Seems a little early in the morning for all that caramel-chocolate-marshmallow whatever."

"It's never too early to Goo Goo."

He walked confidently toward the register. Somehow, I'd forgotten about all the grief I'd caught from Dad the last time I'd hung out with Boone Wyant. But this was breakfast. Full-on daylight. In a public place, surrounded by witnesses.

Surely, this was a different situation altogether.

He grabbed two glass bottles of Coke from a vintage cooler next to the register filled with ice and drinks.

"Candy *and* soda?" I watched him place the bottles on the counter with the Goo Goo Clusters. "Let me guess: 'Dentist' isn't on your list of backup careers."

"I don't have a list of backup careers," he said. "There's only music. That's all I can do. That's all I *am*. So I'm gonna make it, because I have to."

Yes. That was exactly how I felt, too. I always hated when people—always adults, usually men—insisted I needed some kind of backup plan, like my dreams of making it were nothing but dreams. Like it was impossible for anyone to make a living through music. Of course, that wasn't true. I'd watched Dad work as a successful musician my whole life.

But I was going to be a bigger star than Dad. Someday, *everyone* would know the name Josie McCoy.

"You got a couple minutes?" Boone asked, a Biscuit Barrel plastic bag swinging from his wrist.

"A few." Still no sign of Dad or Pauly. "Maybe."

"Come rock with me."

He held open the door, and I walked through, then took a seat in one of the red rocking chairs on the Biscuit Barrel porch that boasted quite the expansive view of the parking lot and the highway beyond it. Really picturesque, postcard-worthy stuff.

Boone settled into the chair next to me; it creaked slightly under his weight. Using the arm of the chair, he knocked off the bottle cap and handed me a Coke. I took a sip, trying to remember the last time I'd had a soda, the dark liquid fizzy and too sweet. He tossed me a candy and it landed neatly in my lap. I ripped open the wrapper and bit in.

"Okay, that's pretty good," I said through a mouthful of Goo Goo. "And here I was, just assuming you'd be at Biscuit Barrel for the biscuits."

"I would never." He shook his head emphatically. "It's Meemaw's biscuits or bust."

"Meemaw?"

"My grandma." He took another bite of Goo Goo Cluster. A little chocolate lingered on his lower lip. "Even though she's supposed to be retired, she still makes all the biscuits for the restaurant. She'd drive up here and tan my hide if she thought I was eating mass-produced biscuits. Bring shame on the family."

"You've got a little something. Right there." I gestured to my lip, and his tongue snuck out to lick on exactly the wrong side. "No, not there." I laughed. "Over here." I gestured again, and he wiped at his lip with his thumb, still wrong. "Come here."

I leaned forward off my rocking chair. With my thumb, I brushed gently along his lower lip.

"There," I said. "Got it."

But I didn't pull away, and neither did he.

"Well, this looks cozy."

"Dad!" Like a shot, I leaned back into my chair. Dad

stood above me, clutching a Biscuit Barrel to-go cup, his fedora pulled low on his brow. Wisely, Pauly walked right by us toward the van, a bulging plastic bag swinging from his wrist.

I really hoped he bought the cardinal-in-a-snow-globe sweater.

"Look who I ran into," I said, gesturing to Boone like I was showing off a prize on a game show. "It's your favorite murderer."

"Your safety isn't a joke, Josie," Dad growled.

"Boone Wyant, sir." Boone leapt up out of the rocking chair and stuck out his hand. "It's an honor to meet you. I'm a big fan. You're our greatest living jazz musician. And I'm not a murderer. Sir."

"Hmm," Dad said, like the jury was still out on that one, but he shook Boone's hand, anyway.

"Boone's going to Pittsburgh, too." I was sort of enjoying watching the two of them face off from the comfort of my rocking chair. Dad's ire was a lot funnier when it wasn't directed at me. Boone was really sweating in that flannel.

"Not because of Josie. Sir. I mean, not that I wouldn't go see your show. But my tour just happened to be booked through Pittsburgh, too. Sir."

"Well, I'm sure whatever honky-tonk has booked you will be grateful for your musical stylings," Dad said dismissively.

"I'm playing the Lonesome Cowboy tomorrow night.

I'd be honored if you and Josie would come to the late show." I had to admire his nerve. If Dad was looking at me the way he was looking at Boone, I wouldn't have invited him anywhere. But also, like, LOL at inviting me somewhere *with my dad*. If this was Boone shooting his shot, he sure went about it differently than the guys back home. "I'll make sure your names are on the list for the good seats. And leave you some drink tickets at the door."

"I'm sober. And thank you so much for offering to ply my eighteen-year-old daughter with alcohol."

"Soda!" Boone squawked. "They have soda!"

It was time to put this nervous white boy out of his misery.

"Okay, Dad." I stood up, placing a calming hand on Dad's arm. "Why don't we get on the road. See you in Pittsburgh, Boone."

Dad harrumphed.

"What do you think, Dad? Should we catch some country music while we're in Pittsburgh?" I teased as we walked toward the van. I knew that was about as likely as Dad opening our next set with "Milkshake."

"If I wanted to hear someone cry into their beer about women and trucks, I'd just ask Pauly about his ex-wife."

That had *not* come up during our many conversations about bees.

As the van pulled out of the parking lot, Boone was back in his rocker, soda in one hand, candy in the other. He lifted up his bottle in a toast, and I waved at him, even though I knew he couldn't see me through the tinted windows. There were a lot of Comfort Motels and Biscuit Barrels in the world, and yet, somehow, we'd ended up in the same place. Twice. I didn't believe in fate—I'd seen too many terrible things happen to good people to think there was some kind of grand design—but it was hard not to wonder why I kept running into him.

I didn't have to wonder why I kept thinking about him, though. There was the killer smile and the broad shoulders and the low voice that churned my insides like butter . . . and . . . well. All of that.

Maybe Kevin would want to go to the Lonesome Cowboy. Surely, Dad couldn't object to me spending a little more time with my favorite stepbrother . . .

I had a good feeling about Pittsburgh.

A *very* good feeling.

CHAPTER TWENTY-ONE
Katy

BRINGING A GARMENT BAG *INTO* Lacy's was definitely a first for me.

Well, not that I'd ever carried *out* one of my own. I'd helped Veronica carry plenty of garment bags out of the store, but all my Lacy's purchases had been more of the something-small-and-inexpensive-enough-to-fit-in-a-tote-bag variety.

Now, clutching my garment bag tightly to my chest, I emerged from the chaos outside into the cool, controlled comfort of Lacy's. Keeping an eye on the elaborate wall clock, desperate not to be late, I hustled past the makeup counters and perfume spritzers, my heels tapping an anxious staccato tempo on the floor.

The shoes had probably been a mistake. I should have worn flats or at least something with a stacked heel, but instead, I'd chosen this pair, with their spindly heels and delicate T-strap, because I wanted to show off the leather-work I'd done on the toe. But they were going to look a lot less impressive if I started limping from my rapidly developing blisters.

I reached the elevator and pressed the button. Luckily, it illuminated immediately, and the doors slid open. Wow. Even the elevators in Lacy's had chandeliers.

God, it was all just perfect.

"Hold the door!"

I turned to see a girl around my age running toward me, long braids flying behind her—very Zoë Kravitz chic. She had a garment bag and a coat slung over her arms. I stuck my arm out to hold the door open, and she slid into the elevator. Up close, I could see the sky-blue suspenders holding up her high-waisted black jeans had little cat faces embroidered on them. They looked too clever to have been commercially made—I wondered if we were going to the same place.

"Thanks," she wheezed, dragging her arm across a bead of sweat on her forehead. "The G train stopped for no reason for *ages*, and I thought I'd never make it in time. Deja Birungi," she introduced herself, freeing one hand from under her garment bag and holding it out to me.

"Katy Keene." I shook it. "Love the suspenders."

"Katy Keene. Felix's replacement. We got an email about you," she said, eyes widening. "Good luck."

"Yep, that's me." I smiled, hoping I looked more confident than I felt. "Do you know what happened to Felix, actually?"

"Nah-unh." She shook her head. "And do *not* ask. They've been very clear that Felix's departure is not up for discussion."

"Got it." I nodded. "Anything else I should know?"

"Normal stuff. Don't be late. Don't bother Rex with the little stuff. Don't talk to anyone official unless they talk to you first."

"Are there official Lacy's people here, too?" Maybe this would turn into a job opportunity more quickly than I'd thought! "Like, is Gloria here? Gloria Grandbilt?"

"Gloria? God, no." She shook her head emphatically. The elevator dinged and we both stepped out onto the sixth floor, into a hallway with cream walls bearing framed black-and-white sketches of fashion designs with '50s silhouettes. I'd never been up to the sixth floor before. "Don't you know? About her and Rex?"

Here's what I knew about Gloria Grandbilt: The woman was an absolute legend. She ran the personal shopping department at Lacy's with a perfectly manicured iron fist. Since she started at Lacy's, she'd been responsible for dressing every celebrity, socialite, and style icon who walked through the doors, and she was also behind the creation of nearly every trend in that time, too. Allegedly, Karl Lagerfeld once said, "If you want to know what everyone will be wearing tomorrow, look at what Gloria Grandbilt is wearing today." There was also a rumor that no one had ever seen her sweat.

Here's what I didn't know about Gloria Grandbilt: whatever Deja was talking about.

Deja leaned closer, her already low voice now pitched to an almost unintelligible volume.

"They *hate* each other," she whispered, looking around like she was worried that the walls had ears at Lacy's. "You know Rex London used to be a personal shopper here?" I nodded. That much I did know—thanks, Veronica. "He was the first male personal shopper Lacy's had ever had, if you can believe that. Gloria really stuck her neck out to get him the job, so the story goes. Mrs. Lacy was against hiring a man, but Gloria said Rex London had the best eye she'd ever seen—apart from her own, of course."

"So what happened?" I whispered back.

"Rex got cast on *Project Catwalk* and quit with no notice. One day, he just didn't show up to his shift. A shift where, by the way, he was supposed to be dressing Tom Hanks for awards season." Deja's eyes widened with significance. "He hadn't pulled the looks he was supposed to, either. Gloria salvaged everything, because she's a genius, but it was almost a disaster. And if Tom Hanks wasn't so nice, it probably would have been a disaster, anyway."

"Yikes." I winced, imagining how stressful that must have been.

"She's never forgiven him for abandoning her like that. And there's never been a man in the personal shopping department since," Deja concluded. "They're all Gloria's Girls, and I do mean that literally. Come on. This way."

"I'm surprised Lacy's is hosting this fashion show for him, then." I followed Deja down the hallway, the black-and-white sketches becoming more modern as we made our way toward wherever we were going.

"Like they were going to turn it down?" Deja snorted derisively. "No way. Rex London is probably the most famous former employee they've ever had. Mrs. Lacy is way too smart to turn down the kind of business a Rex London fashion show is going to bring in. She's just going to keep Gloria safely sequestered on the personal shopping floor. Or maybe she sent her to Paris. Who knows. Either way, I promise you, we're not going to see a single shiny blonde hair on that stylish head."

Huh. That was kind of a disappointment. Part of me had hoped I might meet Gloria and somehow impress her enough to get a job interview, but even if that wasn't an option, I would have loved to just be able to see her.

Deja grabbed a golden door handle and pulled open a set of cream-colored wooden doors. Inside, there was a flurry of activity, most of it centered around a raised dais in front of a three-way mirror. Very *Say Yes to the Dress*. Around the room, other designers brought clothes out of garment bags, hanging them on racks.

There was so much color, so much texture, my eyes could barely focus on any one garment. They bounced from dresses to shirts to pants, everything so impressive. It all looked so professional. I clutched my garment bag a little tighter to my chest, suddenly self-conscious about my dress. How would it compare with everyone else's work?

"Katy Keene?" A man with bright blue hair, glasses,

a clipboard, and a harried expression stood in front of me. "I'm Andy Holtz. Rex London's assistant. We spoke over email?"

"Oh, yes, of course, hi!" Once again, I extricated my arm out from under the garment bag to shake hands, feeling like I was juggling fabric. "I'm Katy. It's so nice to meet you. And thank you so much for this opportunity; it's really incredible—"

"Yes, it is." He cut me off, gushing. "It's an incredible opportunity that literally thousands of designers would kill for. You are so unbelievably lucky to be here! *Everyone* wanted this gig."

"Right." My smile faltered as I thought about the thousands of other designers who wanted to be here. "Well, I'm definitely very grateful—"

"You're a hard person to vet, Katy Keene," he said teasingly, waving a finger at me. "You don't have much of a social media presence. Most of these other designers have quite a substantial following. Your Instagram is set to *private*."

"Oh. I, um, didn't realize that was a problem." I did a mental catalog of my Instagram, which definitely did include some outfit-of-the-day posts featuring clothes I'd made, but also included a lot of selfies of me and KO, blurry videos of Jorge dancing at Molly's Crisis, and a very thorough documentation of my quest for the best slice of ninety-nine-cent pizza in the city. It didn't exactly scream *professional designer.*

"Oh, it isn't!" he rushed to reassure me. "Not necessarily. It just made it very hard to discern whether or not you were the caliber of designer Rex would feel confident putting in a show that he attached his name to." His eyes bored into my garment bag like he was trying to see its contents with X-ray vision. I clutched it even tighter, protective of my poor dress. "But don't worry! I'm sure it's great. The word of Veronica Lodge is good enough for Rex, so it's good enough for me."

He was smiling at me, but somehow his unrelenting enthusiasm was just making me *more* nervous. I felt so cute when I left the house in this polka dot dress and cropped navy blazer this morning, but now I felt wrinkly and sweaty. Not Rex London material.

"Right," he said. "Find a place on the rack and get set up. Can't wait to see what you've got! And don't worry if it needs a couple tweaks. Rex understands that everyone else has had weeks to fine-tune their designs with him."

Exactly what I *didn't* need to be reminded of, but I smiled brightly at Andy one last time, anyway, before he buzzed off toward another unsuspecting designer. I would be professional and pleasant if it killed me. My smile feeling brittle, I hung my garment bag on the rolling rack nearest the door, but before I got out my dress, I couldn't resist pulling out my phone. Did everyone here really have a huge Instagram following? A quick search of Deja Birungi pulled up her account and all eighteen thousand of her followers. Holy cow. I scrolled through her feed, full of gorgeous, quirky looks and expertly tailored pants. Thank goodness my Instagram *was* set to private. In comparison, it was kind of embarrassing.

Back on my feed, I noticed KO had posted a new photo. It was a black-and-white shot of Jinx in the boxing gym, her gloves framing her model-perfect face, a single bead of sweat dripping down the side of her forehead, like it had been painted there by an art director. It was a beautiful shot, the interplay of darkness and light adding curves and shadows to the already gorgeous planes of Jinx's face. KO had captioned it "Killer Queen."

I looked back at my Instagram. We'd both been so busy, with this Rex London fashion show and KO's time at the boxing gym, there weren't any recent photos of me and KO together. I had to scroll back quite a bit to find a picture of the two of us at Coney Island this summer, attempting to Lady and the Tramp a Nathan's Famous hot dog, with very poor results. I had mustard in one of my eyebrows, but I looked radiantly happy.

But since then, we'd done no leaf peeping, no pumpkin patching, no apple picking.

I knew we still had plenty of time for those things . . . but I missed him. Would we ever get the chance to *really* start our best fall ever?

"Katy?" Andy was back in front of me, still smiling, but it didn't quite meet his eyes. "I'm sorry, are we keeping you from something important on your phone? Do you need to step out into the hallway?"

"No! Oh my gosh, no! I'm sorry, I was just—I'm just sorry." My cheeks flamed with embarrassment. *Wow, really professional, Katy.* Quickly, I shoved my phone back into my cross-body bag, where I vowed it would stay, permanently, and unzipped the garment bag—like my skills at speed-unzipping could somehow make up for the poor first impression I'd made.

"Designers!" I turned to the doors. Rex London was instantly recognizable, with his tan skin, dark eyebrows, and signature pouf of silver hair. He was even shorter in real life than I'd thought he was, but his slim three-piece suit was perfectly tailored. Most people wouldn't pair a plaid suit with a floral button-down, but on Rex London, it just *worked*.

"He's a genius, isn't he?" Deja was back at my side, whispering, her eyes glowing with admiration. "I *aspire* to that level of pattern-mixing greatness. Just watching what he puts together for his own look every day has been a master class."

I nodded happily. There was a glow around Rex London. I wasn't sure if it was the special sort of buzz that changed in the air around a celebrity—like that time Jorge and I saw Sarah Jessica Parker walking down Christopher Street and we almost fell off the stoop we'd been sitting on—or if he was just so well-moisturized that it was coming from his skin.

"Today, we're doing our last look on the racks, and then we'll start fitting." Rex placed his hands in front of his mouth, almost like he was praying. "Let's get these looks ready to walk, people!"

Fitting! This was so exciting. I'd never worked with a professional model before. I'd only ever made clothes for me or my friends.

"When are the models coming?" I asked Deja, grateful that I hadn't missed any of the fittings with them. Maybe I wouldn't be as behind as I'd feared!

"What are you talking about, Katy?" Deja tilted her head quizzically. "*We're* the models."

CHAPTER TWENTY-TWO
Jorge

"JORGE!" KATY FLEW THROUGH THE door of Molly's Crisis, her red silk scarf trailing behind her like a flame. That girl understood the importance of a personal brand. Not that Katy would have ever described herself as having a personal brand, but she had a look that was all her own. Very retro-cutie-Eleganza. Like Minnie Mouse's more sophisticated big sister. "I'm having a crisis!"

"No better place to have one." I smirked. "I wonder what Molly's original crisis was?"

Even if anyone knew the answer to that, there was nobody here to tell me. I looked around the empty bar. Technically, they weren't open yet, but the door had been unlocked. Seriously, somebody needed to give me Darius's job. If I ever left the bodega unlocked when we were closed, the *New York Post* would run a story titled "Bodega Bloodshed!" because Ma would literally murder me.

"Maybe it was getting a once-in-a-lifetime spot in a fashion show and then realizing *she* had to *model* her own designs!"

"OMG, Katy-girl, are you serious?!" I couldn't keep the excitement off my face, even though Katy looked panicked. "I love this for you!"

"Well, I don't love this for me! I hate this for me!" As she started taking off her navy blazer, I realized the buttons were tiny strawberries. She was too cute.

"Are these new?" I tapped a strawberry button. "I'm living for them."

"Yes, I was digging around at Lou Lou Buttons and I couldn't resist. It really transforms the jacket, doesn't it? But forget the strawberries!" She dropped her coat on the bar stool, revealing a red silk dress with tiny white polka dots, puffed sleeves, and fabric-covered buttons marching all the way down the front. That Katy Keene look, perfect as always. "I can't do this! I'm not a model!"

"Okay, you're not a model, but you *can* do this." I plucked the umbrella out of my ginger ale, then tucked it into her hair, behind her ear. "It's just walking, Katy. You can walk."

"In a casual way! Not a professional, runway, fashion kind of way! With everyone looking at me!"

"They won't be looking at *you*, they'll be looking at your dress. That's what matters. And forget the modeling for a second. What did Rex London think about your dress?"

"My dress. Oh my god. My dress." She face-palmed

herself. "I left it at Lacy's. I don't even know if I was supposed to. I was just so preoccupied I forgot about it."

"Girl, did you just run out of there in a panic after they told you that *you* were going to model?" I frowned. "That's not a great look."

"No, I didn't panic run!" She leaned over to take a sip of my ginger ale. "They ended up cutting the fitting short today. Rex had some kind of emergency with the filming of his makeover show and had to leave early. He hasn't even seen my dress yet."

"Well, he's gonna love it, whenever he sees it. And why haven't *I* seen it yet?" I demanded. Usually, Katy always showed me what she was working on, every step of the way. "I thought you'd at least text me a pic of the finished product."

"Yeah, I will." She avoided my eyes guiltily. "I just . . . I don't know. I'm still not feeling sure about it. Maybe I should go back uptown to Lacy's to grab it, so I can tinker around with it a little bit before Rex sees it."

"Don't tinker too much. Remember what Coco Chanel said about taking off one accessory before leaving the house. Or what I said before the homecoming dance freshman year."

"I still can't believe I thought *fingerless gloves* were a good idea." Katy shook her head.

"Even the fashion greats make mistakes. And you're gonna be one the greats. So text me a picture of that dress, please!" She nodded. I hoped she would. I wasn't used to seeing Katy lacking confidence, especially when it came to the clothes she made. She was so good, and usually, she knew it. "In the meantime, cover girl, let's put some bass in your walk."

"I don't know how to put some bass in my walk. I don't even know what that means." Katy dropped her head into her hands, moaning. "I am so screwed."

I skipped over to the sound system in the back. They *should* just give me a job here; I knew where everything was. Despite having grown up above our bodega, I had a feeling my own special set of skills was suited more to song selections and serving drinks than frying egg sandwiches and selling Flamin' Hot Cheetos to the kids from PS 187. Maybe they'd even let me sing. Sometimes, they had performers who weren't in drag.

And hey, if I was a Broadway star, they'd probably be *begging* me to sing.

After my last callback, though, that was a big *if*. Ethan Fox's comments wouldn't stop rolling around in my head. Like, I knew he was the director, and it was his vision, and ultimately, it was a commentary on the *character*, not on *me*, but it still felt personal. Too personal.

Like *I* was the problem, not my performance.

I still hadn't decided if I was going back for the next round of callbacks. And if I did go back, would I try it more masc? Steal some clothes from one of my brothers and give them exactly what I knew they wanted? Or would I still read it the way *I* saw Barnaby?

It felt like way too big of an opportunity to just give up. This was literally everything I ever wanted, and the director was rooting for me. He *wanted* it to be me— literally. Things like this didn't happen to kids fresh out of high school, but somehow, it was happening for me.

I plugged my phone into the auxiliary cord and scrolled through Spotify until I found "Vogue." Sometimes, the classics were classic for a reason.

Madonna blasted through the speakers. Katy looked perkier already. She snapped along with the song as she followed me up onto the stage.

"Strike a pose," I instructed, along with Madonna.

"Vogue," Katy whispered back to me, framing her face with her hands.

"Definitely don't do that, though," I said. "Pretty sure literally vogueing is frowned upon in high fashion circles."

"I know *that* at least." She rolled her eyes, smiling. "I'm not that hopeless."

"Pretend this is the runway." I held on to Katy's shoulder and steered her stage left, turning her until she faced the wings backstage right. The stage at Molly's Crisis was too narrow to walk toward the audience, but it would work this way. "Now, pick a point to focus on. Stand tall, keep your limbs loose, place one foot in front of the other, and walk with long strides."

I was so glad my summer of bingeing reality TV had

paid off. Between watching *Project Catwalk* and *America's Next Super Model* and *Drag Race*, I was practically an amateur runway coach at this point.

Katy stomped down the faux-runway like an adorably tiny T. rex.

"Relax your hands!" I shouted. She flared them out like she was attempting a casual jazz hand, then she balled them into fists, then she cupped them like a Barbie.

It was . . . not great.

"Why are my hands so weird?" She waved them at me, flailing, once she hit the other side of the stage. "Have my hands always been so weird? Why didn't you tell me I had weird hands, Jorge?!"

Maybe if I tried to walk myself, I could help her. I picked a point backstage, focused, set my shoulders, and walked forward, channeling all the reality TV goddesses I'd watched this summer.

"No, no, no!" Darius emerged from backstage, wearing a short silk robe over his padding. His face was beat for the gods, but he still had on a wig cap. Maybe this was what it would look like if Taye Diggs did drag. I bet he'd be gorgeous. "Shut this down!" Darius faced us, hands on his hip. "There will be no gay-best-friend-teaches-straight-girl-to-runway-walk-at-the-drag-bar music montage today!"

"We're having a crisis, Darius!" I protested. "A Molly's Crisis!"

"That doesn't even mean anything!"

"Help, please." With those big eyes, Katy looked like a sad kitten.

"Oh, fine." Darius sighed heavily. "But shut this sad little walk-off down before any real customers come in. We don't want to scare them off."

"Was it really that bad?" Katy asked once Darius disappeared back toward the dressing room. "Like, scaring-paying-customers-off bad?"

"It wasn't so much 'bad' as it was 'good-adjacent,'" I said diplomatically. Katy groaned. "But you can turn this out. Come on. Show me that Katy Keene can-do spirit!"

As we walked the stand-in runway on the Molly's Crisis stage, my phone cycling through Madonna's greatest hits, I felt free. Free to make things more *me*, to move through the space the way I wanted to, without worrying about how masc I looked. And I could almost get Ethan Fox's words out of my head.

Almost.

CHAPTER TWENTY-THREE
Pepper

"SO YOU FINALLY CAME TO see me." Ms. Freesia took a sip of her tea, the gold rim of the elegant china cup a stark contrast with her perfectly painted crimson lips. "I was beginning to think you were avoiding me."

"Don't be silly." I placed the box of macarons I'd picked up at Ladurée especially for her on the coffee table, a peace offering. "I would never."

"Ooh, my favorite." She clapped her hands girlishly. "I hope you brought plenty of the black currant–violet ones."

"Of course. I know what you like."

"Well, you've been gone for so long, *ma petite chou*, I wouldn't be surprised at all if you'd forgotten everything about me." Ms. Freesia sniffed dramatically, like some disconsolate grande dame on Broadway.

"There's no need for theatrics." I sniffed right back at her. Ivan, Ms. Freesia's cat, jumped into her lap. He was an ugly thing, totally hairless, with large, bat-like ears, but she adored him. Ivan narrowed his eyes at me, blinking, like he was plotting some kind of nasty surprise. "I've simply been busy."

"Busy with what? Your latest blonde floozy?"

"Not a floozy. You'd like her, actually." I felt a smile I couldn't resist playing about my lips. "She can definitely handle herself, that one."

"Ooh. Who is she?" Ms. Freesia asked eagerly. "Heiress? Hedge fund manager? CEO of a Silicon Valley start-up?"

"Not everything is about money, you know."

"It's like I've taught you nothing." She shook her head at me, but she was laughing.

"Well, it's lovely to see you back here at the Georgia."

"It's a lovely building. I can assure you, Ms. Freesia, if I ever decide to join a co-op, I'd only consider buying at the Georgia."

"It is the only address worth having in New York, and it has been since Grace Kelly maintained her Manhattan home here."

"Back in the days when you and Princess Grace were old school chums?"

"I'm not that old." Ms. Freesia's eyes narrowed. I knew I shouldn't tease, but sometimes it was awfully satisfying to get a rise out of the old girl. "So what's the plan, Pepper? What are you going to do next?"

"I haven't quite decided yet." I took a macaron from the box—not one of the black currant-violet ones—and took a bite. That was the question everyone kept asking, but I simply wasn't sure where I wanted to direct my energies and tremendous talents.

"Well, whenever you do decide, darling, let me know." She smiled warmly. "Include me in whatever plans you have. I'm here for you always. I hope you know that."

"I do, Ms. Freesia. I do."

But what *were* my plans? The longer I stayed in New York, the more pressure I felt to launch my next big venture. The press had been nothing but kind since I arrived, but I knew they could turn on me in an instant. Being *Pepper Smith* meant something, and one of the things it meant was that I couldn't rest on my (admittedly impressive) laurels. You were only as good as your next great idea, and I needed mine.

Of course, I always had Ms. Freesia and her trusty black book to turn to, but I was hoping it wouldn't come to that.

Whatever I did next, I wanted to do it on my own.

CHAPTER TWENTY-FOUR
Josie

I KNEW THE OLD JOKE about how you get to Carnegie Hall: practice, practice, practice. But it turns out you can also get to Carnegie Hall by driving into Pittsburgh while on tour with your dad. Doesn't have quite the same ring to it, though.

The room they'd given me to get ready in wasn't quite like dressing rooms I was used to seeing. It was a big open space on the second floor, full of a random assortment of Victorian-looking furniture and a few full-length mirrors scattered around, leaning against the walls. I examined my reflection in one of these mirrors, adjusting the halter neckline of my black jumpsuit. Turning my head this way and that, my silver chandelier earrings nearly brushed my bare shoulders.

"Josie, you are looking good tonight," I addressed my reflection. Well, I guessed the natural next stop after only talking to Dad and Pauly was to start talking to myself.

But unlike Pauly, I didn't even know any interesting facts about bees. I thought again about sneaking out with Kevin to see Boone's late show after my gig tonight. But that was a ridiculous thought. After what Dad said last time he caught me sneaking out? Boone wasn't worth the risk.

Someone knocked on the door. I glanced up at the wall clock—way too early to start the show. Curious, I crossed to the door, and opened it to find my dad waiting for me.

"Hey, Josie." He pushed up the brim of his fedora and scratched at his forehead. "Really exciting news." If he was excited, I sure couldn't tell. That man had elevated the poker face to an art form. "We're adding a new stop to the tour. We're taking a detour to New York."

"New York? New York City?" I squealed, hoping he wasn't about to say we were actually heading to Buffalo, New York. No offense to Buffalo, obviously—god bless the inventors of the buffalo wing—but it didn't have quite the same cachet as New York City, especially when it came to performing.

"It's a little out of the way, but I just heard from the booker at Tiny's."

Tiny's. *Oh my god.* Tiny's was a legendary jazz club in the Village. *Everyone* who was anyone had played there, and now I was about to become one of those exclusive everyones?

"Their headliner canceled, and they knew I was out on the road," Dad continued. "So we'll be heading there tomorrow."

"Tiny's. Wow, Dad." I couldn't quite believe it. "That's *awesome.*"

"It is awesome," he deadpanned. "You never know who could be in the audience. Agents, bookers, managers, talent scouts . . ." This could be my big break. A chance for me to go solo. "You need to be perfect, Josie. The name Myles McCoy means something. I can't have you embarrassing me."

"I wouldn't." I bristled. He thought I would *embarrass* him? Every time I thought I'd proved myself to my dad, by turning out stellar performances night after night, he'd pull something like this. It made me feel all of five years old again, listening to Dad critique my performance of "Rainbow Connection" at the kindergarten talent show as "a little pitchy."

"Just keep on top of the tempo, okay? I'm still not happy with that bridge."

"Got it." I gritted my teeth. The inner metronome strikes again.

"And maybe do a couple more warm-ups tonight that focus on articulation?" he suggested. "Your consonants are getting a little sloppy."

"Great suggestion." I hit the *t* in "great" harder than was necessary.

"I'm just trying to help, Josie." He sighed with exasperation. "The world will be a lot harsher than I am."

"That's kind of hard to believe," I muttered.

"If you want to make it in this business, you need to be

perfect. Better than perfect. And if you can't handle criticism, you should have stayed at home in Riverdale, singing in a diner basement."

Veronica would *not* have appreciated the way he dismissed La Bonne Nuit, and I didn't, either. But it wasn't worth getting into with him.

"I can handle it, Dad."

"Prove it, then. Let's have another great show tonight." He waved, and then turned to head down the stairs. "See you out there."

It was so hard to keep my cool around him. Maybe he did just have my best interests at heart, but it was so much harder being critiqued by Dad than by other people. There was too much baggage there. Trying to calm down, I closed the door and crossed back into the room, taking a seat in a squashy armchair upholstered in red brocade. You know who was the only person who would appreciate this room? Kevin. With all this old, red-upholstered furniture, it looked like the Blossoms were running an estate sale. I missed having someone who got the weirdness of growing up in Riverdale—the more of America I saw, the more it confirmed my belief that my hometown was definitely not normal.

I knew I'd see him tonight, but it couldn't wait. I pulled my phone out of my pocket, scrolled through my contacts until I hit the *K*s, and FaceTimed Kevin.

"Josie?" His familiar face filled the screen, and I realized I'd missed him more than I'd thought.

"Why, if it isn't Kevin Keller!" I cheered. "How's my favorite stepbrother?"

"Happy to see you. Have you forgotten all about the little people from back home, now that you're a big star?"

"Hardly. I could never forget you. Now, look at this couch." I flipped the camera around so Kevin could see what I was pointing at. "What does this remind you of?"

"Oh my god," he said. "I think Nana Rose has that exact same sofa at Thistlehouse."

"Right?" I flipped the camera back to me excitedly. "That's exactly what I thought! I think this place's interior decorator was a Blossom."

"Had to be. Please don't play with fire. We know their taste in decor tends to be extremely flammable."

"Oh my god, Kev, that is too soon." I laughed anyway, though. "I can't wait to see you tonight!"

"Tonight?" he repeated, confused.

"Yeah . . ." Why was he being so weird? "I'm in Pittsburgh. Didn't you get the ticket I emailed you?"

"Oh no." Kevin smacked his face with one hand. "I can't believe this. I completely forgot. I'm not in Pittsburgh."

"What? Where are you?" My fun night out at the Lonesome Cowboy with Kevin was slipping through my fingers like smoke. Now that it wasn't going to happen, I realized just how badly I'd wanted to see him, wanted to have that little piece of home with me out here on the road.

"I'm in New York! I took the train down for this big open call for a show on Broadway," he said, emphasizing the *way*, one jazz hand flared out and framing his handsome face.

"Kevin! Are you serious? That's amazing!" I snapped as he took a series of little bows. "Don't get me wrong, you were a great director for all those musicals back at Riverdale High, but I always thought a voice like yours deserved to be heard *onstage*, too."

"Coming from the greatest diva in the history of Riverdale—and I mean that as nothing but a compliment—"

"I know you do," I interrupted him.

"That really means something," he finished. "Thanks, Josie."

"So? When will I be seeing you on the Great White Way?" I tucked my knees into my chest, getting comfortable.

"Never." He frowned. "Or at least, not anytime soon. I got cut after callbacks."

"Those idiots." I scoffed.

"They said they were looking for someone with more 'edge.'" He air-quoted.

"More edge than you?" I raised an eyebrow. "Did you tell them you survived an organ-harvesting cult?"

"You know, I forgot to mention that." Kevin pursed his lips. "Maybe I should have put that on my 'special skills,' in between 'advanced tap' and 'conversational Spanish.'"

I laughed.

"But seriously, Kevin, even making it to callbacks is a

huge accomplishment," I said. "Maybe you should think about moving to New York after you graduate. Giving Broadway a real shot."

"Why? Are *you* moving to New York?"

I paused. I hadn't really thought about it seriously. It would be nice to have a place to put down roots. Make some friends. And I couldn't imagine anywhere better than New York. I'd never spent any real time there—but I knew it was a city bursting with opportunity.

"I don't know. But I know I'll be there tomorrow. Wait a minute—this is perfect!" I squealed. "We can meet there!"

"I wish I could, Josie, but I have to get back to Carnegie Mellon." Kevin's face fell. "I'm at Penn Station right now, about to get on a train."

"Seriously?" I couldn't believe we were literally swapping places. "Can't you stay for just one more day?" I wheedled.

"I can't. I've already missed so many classes, and I have to give a presentation on the emergence of Noh theater in fourteenth-century Japan tomorrow that's a quarter of my grade."

"Okay, college boy. I understand." I didn't really—I wasn't even sure what Noh theater *was*—but I got that he had other commitments.

"But have fun in New York!" he said encouragingly. "You're gonna love it. And break a leg tonight!"

"Thanks, boo."

I hung up, then stuck the phone back in my bag. No

Kevin. Back to talking to myself. We were just a few minutes to places; I might as well save the stagehand the walk upstairs.

It was a good show; technically perfect, even, but I felt like there was something missing. Like some of the soul I usually sang with was gone. I guess my conversation with Dad was weighing on me. Or maybe it was my disappointment about not seeing Kevin. Usually, singing was my escape, my way out of my head, but I just couldn't get there tonight.

Luckily, the audience didn't seem to notice. Once again, the house wasn't full, but at least the people who were there seemed to love it. It was always gratifying to see a crowd rise to their feet, and I basked in the warmth of the applause as I bowed, a couple steps behind Dad, as always.

"Josie, hold up." I braced myself for Dad's critique, wondering if he could feel the lack of something that I felt tonight. "Would you care to join me at the Lonesome Cowboy for the late show?"

He had to be kidding. I just couldn't figure out *why* he was kidding.

"Is this a joke?" I asked. "Because if it is, it's a weird one."

"Not a joke. I'm interested in looking at this Boone Wyant person as a potential opener for Southern venues. Our tour routes seem to be constantly overlapping—he may be easy to slot into the tour. Pauly pointed out that it might be interesting to have a country artist open for us as we get closer to Nashville." Pauly walked by just then and winked at me. Unbelievable. Was he *matchmaking* me and Boone Wyant?!

"So? Josie?" Dad prompted. I had zoned out for a minute, staring where the winking Pauly had been, unable to process what was happening. My brain was scrambled like I'd just taken Fizzle Rocks. "Would you like to come?"

"Sure. I mean, definitely beats seeing what's in the vending machine at the Comfort Motel Pittsburgh."

"We'll see. The vending machine may end up being preferable to whatever we're about to hear at the Lonesome Cowboy."

"Nice to see you're approaching the evening with your trademark optimism, Dad." I walked past him toward the stairs. "Are you sure you want to ask Boone to come on tour with us? Because it sure doesn't sound like it."

"No. I'm not sure at all. Which is why we're going to hear him sing before we make any decisions."

"Got it. Let me just grab my stuff and I'll meet you out front."

After flying up the stairs, I pulled on my coat, shoved my makeup into my bag, and scrambled back down again, worried that if I took too long, Dad might change his mind. Not because I was excited to see Boone again, obviously, but because I wanted a change of pace from another night alone in a motel.

Or at least that's what I told myself, anyway.

Outside, Pauly and Dad were waiting in the van. I hopped in, and we sped through Pittsburgh, past lots of brick, industrial-looking buildings. In just a few minutes, we pulled up outside the Lonesome Cowboy. The bar's name was spelled out in neon lights, and a huge crowd milled around on the sidewalk. *Had all these people come to see Boone?*

Dad and I climbed out of the van and waited on the sidewalk. There was a lot of flannel and denim in front of us. In our all-black ensembles, we looked like we'd come from a very different party.

Which, I suppose, we had.

"You coming, Pauly?" I opened the door and popped my head back into the van to ask him.

"Nah." He turned over his shoulder to look at me. "I'm going to Primanti's to grab a bite. Get this, Josie—they put the fries *inside* the sandwich."

"What a world we live in, Pauly."

"That we do, Josie, that we do." He waved, and then the van pulled away from the curb.

Dad and I squeezed our way into the crowd, fighting through it until we reached the door. There was a palpable energy in the air, something almost electric.

"Sorry, folks," the bouncer said. "Venue's at capacity. Totally sold out for the late show."

"I think we're on the list," I piped up before Dad could say anything. "Josie and Myles McCoy."

Skeptically, the bouncer flipped through the papers on his clipboard, until, eyebrows raised, he found what he was looking for.

"So you are." He pushed open the door. "Come on in, folks."

Inside, it was absolutely jam-packed. Sure, it was a smaller venue than most of the ones we'd been playing on tour, but none of ours had felt so full, or so alive. You got the sense that a dance party could break out any minute.

"This way, Josie."

I followed Dad. He'd managed to locate a spot for us in the back, not far from the bar. Crowds always did have a way of parting for Myles McCoy. It was something in the way he carried himself.

Not long after we'd settled in against the wall, the lights dimmed. Someone introduced him, and then Boone Wyant walked out, waving, a huge smile on his face, his guitar slung over his back.

"How we doin' tonight, Pittsburgh?" The crowd roared its approval. A very female-sounding approval. I looked to my left, and to my right, and all I saw was long hair and short shorts, despite the decidedly cool temperatures outside. There was no doubt about it: The Boone Wyant fan base was predominantly female. I wondered how many of the girls in the crowd would have happily been his sweetie or darlin' or whatever.

Most of them, probably. I couldn't blame them. He

looked even better under the stage lights than he did in motel lobbies or truck stops or Biscuit Barrels. He was wearing a tight white T-shirt and jeans, nothing special at all, but on him, it just *worked*.

"We're gonna start tonight off with a cover written by probably the greatest songwriter in the history of country music: Miss Dolly Parton."

I smiled. I'd read an article a while ago about the lack of female representation in country, how most radio stations wouldn't play two female artists back-to-back because they thought their listeners would change the dial. It made me like him even more, knowing that he gave Queen Dolly the respect she deserved.

It was a slow, stripped-down cover of "Do I Ever Cross Your Mind." Boone closed his eyes as he crooned into the microphone, the lyrics plaintive. His voice was rich and low, with only a hint of growl that made it all the more irresistible. This boy could *sing*.

Dad nudged my shoulder, breaking the spell.

"Do you think he owns any slacks that aren't denim?" Dad whispered.

I grinned. I knew exactly what that meant.

Boone Wyant was joining the tour.

CHAPTER TWENTY-FIVE
Katy

I LOCKED THE DOOR OF my apartment and turned to see Mr. Discenza down at the end of the hallway. Silently, I pivoted on my heels, hoping I could duck back inside before he saw me.

"Katy!" he called.

No such luck.

"Hi, Mr. Discenza." I winced, knowing exactly what this was about.

"I really need that rent check, Katy." Yup. Exactly what I thought it was about. "You're a good kid, and I know you've been through a lot this year, so I don't want to badger you, but it's ten days overdue."

"I know. I'm sorry. I really am. You know what? Hold on." Unlocking the door, I popped back into the apartment, grabbed the checkbook out of the junk drawer, and quickly scribbled on it. This would be fine. Things would be a little tight for the rest of the month, but at least the check wouldn't bounce. "Here you go." Breathlessly, I emerged into the hall and handed over the check. "It'll be on time next month, I promise. I'm getting a job. I mean, I'm working on getting a job."

I had to work a little harder on finding gainful employment. It was so easy to get swept up in the fashion show, but that didn't pay in anything but experience and exposure. The rent was still due every month, and I needed money coming in, immediately. Back to GregsList tonight. Something would turn up. It had to.

"I'm not sure how many months we'll have left." Mr. Discenza frowned sympathetically. "I have to tell you, Katy, I've been getting an awful lot of interesting offers. I think I'm going to sell the building."

"Do you know when?" I knew this was coming, but my heart sank anyway. Finding an apartment without a job wasn't going to be an easy feat. Maybe I could crash at Jorge's, now that his brothers had all moved out. Or KO's mom would definitely let me stay on their pullout couch in the living room, but there were too many Kellys to have me underfoot indefinitely. Plus, the commute in from Long Island might kill me. I was a Manhattan girl, thank you very much.

"Not sure yet, but I promise I'll give you plenty of notice. Even more than thirty days if I can."

"Thanks, Mr. Discenza." I smiled wanly. "I appreciate it."

And I *did* appreciate the heads-up, although that wouldn't make things any easier. New York real estate was a nightmare, but I knew I'd just been prolonging the inevitable. At first, I'd been afraid of leaving the only apartment I'd ever known, afraid that would make me feel further from Mom, but the idea of a fresh start had some appeal. No matter where I went, Mom would always be with me. Especially as long as I had her sewing machine, it was like she was always right by my side as I worked.

Realistically, I couldn't really afford to stay here, anyway. I needed a more affordable neighborhood, and a roommate. Or two.

I walked down the four flights of stairs to the front door. A familiar figure was sitting on our front stoop. Grinning broadly, I flew down the stairs, flung my arms around his neck, and covered his cheeks in kisses.

"Boy, I really hope this is Katy, otherwise I've got some unfortunate news for Mrs. Discenza," KO joked. "How's the most gorgeous girl on Delancey Street doing this morning?" He grabbed ahold of my arms and squeezed.

"Better, now that I've seen you. What are you doing here?" I held out my hands and pulled him up to his feet. "Why didn't you tell me you were coming?"

"I wanted to surprise you. And I brought breakfast." He bent down to pick up a bag.

"Ooh!" Eagerly, I dug into the bag, ripped the foil off a breakfast sandwich, and bit in, the cheese hot and gooey. "Yum." I sighed lustily. "You know the way to my heart,"

I said through a big mouthful. "You plus cheese is the best surprise a girl could ask for."

"I thought you might need some cheese. You seemed sort of stressed when we talked last night." (KO and I said goodnight to each other over the phone every night. We'd been doing it since we were sixteen. I know, I know, we were totally dorky, but I loved it.)

"I *am* sort of stressed." We walked down the stairs holding hands. The beauty of the breakfast sandwich was that I could eat *and* hold hands. KO always knew exactly what I needed. "Did you get yourself a sandwich?"

"I, uh, ate it already." He blushed. KO had many virtues, but patience where food was involved was not one of them. "What's stressing you out? The modeling thing?"

"Yes, the modeling thing." I wished I could think about it the way KO said it, like it was no big deal.

"What's the problem? Katy, you could be a model. You're literally the most beautiful person I've ever seen."

"That is so sweet, KO, but you're biased."

"No way. I'm totally objective. I don't mind telling you, for example, that your feet are like icicles, and you sneeze so loudly it's a little scary, and you're really terrible at finding your way around Long Island. You've been to my house about a billion times, yet somehow, you still always get lost."

"Well, thanks for cataloging my faults." I laughed, punching him on the arm. "But that last one's not on me.

That's Long Island's fault. It needs a nice, neat grid system. Like Manhattan."

"There you go again, with your borough snobbery," he teased. He let go of my hand to check his phone. "But I have to be honest, Katy, I don't see what the big deal is about the modeling thing."

"It's a *huge* deal!" I exclaimed. "I swear, I'm not saying this to fish for compliments, but I'm not a model. And it's not even about how I look. I'm not meant to be in the spotlight! Like, sure, I'm always happy to do karaoke with Jorge, but that's different, because we're doing something fun, together. And Jorge really carries the weight. He could sing next to a potted plant and make it look like a star. No, I'm more of a behind-the-scenes girl. Like, I love the idea of people seeing my clothes—that's all I've ever wanted—but I don't need anyone to see *me* in them. I mean, think about it." I crumpled up my tinfoil and tossed it into a trash can, pausing for a moment while the light changed before we crossed the street. "Seriously. Would *you* want to be a model? I know you're used to being in front of crowds while you're boxing, but you're doing something. You're focused on the match, and your opponent. Now imagine you're just standing there, in the middle of the ring, walking back and forth, and everyone's looking at you, and judging you, and I . . . KO?" I trailed off as I turned around and realized KO wasn't next to me anymore. I was walking alone and talking to myself. Luckily, nobody else on the sidewalk seemed to think that was weird.

You had to love the anonymity of New York. There was something so peaceful about it. I was pretty sure there was nowhere else on earth you could openly weep in public and no one would bother you. Every once in a while, a girl just needed a good subway cry. Before I met KO, Jorge and I had both had a crush on this guy in our math class, and when it turned out he didn't like either of us, Jorge and I had cried almost the entire length of Broadway, and nobody said anything.

So, yes, points to New York for its crowds that guaranteed emotional anonymity, but curse those crowds for making it hard to locate a missing boxer boyfriend. I rose up on my tiptoes, trying to spot KO. A man in a suit brushed past me, causing me to stumble, cursing under his breath about people stopping in the middle of the sidewalk.

Retracing my steps, I crossed back over the street, and finally spotted KO, smiling at his phone while standing outside an eyebrow-threading place.

"KO?" I asked, planting my feet firmly in front of him. "Hello? KO?" I tapped him on the bridge of his nose.

"Huh?" Finally he looked up, blinking, like he was surprised to see me there.

"Everything okay?" I asked. "I lost you for a couple of blocks."

"Aw, man, I'm sorry, Katy. Jinx texted me, and I—" He looked back down at the phone and started laughing. "Oh man. This girl cracks me up. I'd explain it, but it's a whole boxing thing—"

"Don't worry about it," I reassured him, but I was kind of worried. I didn't think KO was cheating on me—I knew he would *never* do that—but I still felt jealous that some other girl was making him laugh so hard he forgot he was walking with me and ended up stranded by a threading place. It felt like there was now this whole new part of his life that I wasn't part of. Or, I guess, more accurately, it felt like he now had someone who understood one of the most important parts of his life better than I could.

I always tried my best to support KO's boxing career, but I didn't really get it. I knew the basic gist of all the rules and I'd sparred with KO a couple of times, for fun, but I didn't get the appeal. The boxing gloves smelled like BO and throwing punches hurt my hands. Just like KO wasn't at home in the fashion world, I knew nothing about life in the ring. And I'd never thought that was a problem before—but now?

I wasn't so sure.

"So what were you saying?" KO tucked his phone back into his pocket. "About the fashion show?"

"Nothing." I didn't really feel like getting into it again. "Just stressing out about the modeling stuff. It's not important."

"If it's stressing you out, it *is* important." I couldn't even be mad at him for not listening. He was so sweet. "But maybe what you need is a break. Listen. I didn't come down here just to bring you breakfast. Why don't we hop on the train and go to that apple orchard you told me about?

Look, I even wore my most fabulous fall shirt." I smiled. It *was* a very nice plaid. "We can walk around, share some cider, pick some apples. Take them back to Mom's and bake a pie or something."

"Can you bake a pie?"

"I'm sure I could figure it out." He grinned. Out of the two us, KO definitely had more skills in the kitchen. Right now, I was using my oven to store pattern-making paper: a terrible, extremely flammable idea. "Might be nice to forget about the fashion show for a little while and do something fun, just the two of us."

"Oh, KO, I wish I could." That sounded like exactly the kind of escape I needed. "But I can't. We have the fitting."

"I thought that was yesterday." He frowned.

"It was." I frowned right back at him. "Rex London cut the fitting short and then had to reschedule it for today, remember? I told you about it. Last night. I'm on my way there right now. Where did you think we were walking?"

"Right, right." KO rubbed his hand over his forehead. "Sorry, Katy. I should have remembered. I was out so late with Jinx last night I was kind of zonked."

"Right," I said tightly. I hadn't realized KO had been out with Jinx. We'd had our goodnight call later than usual, but I'd thought that had been because I'd been panic-binge-watching old episodes of *Project Catwalk*, trying to pick up some tips, not because KO had been out with another girl.

"I promise you, Katy. We will make it to the apple

orchard." He took both of my hands in his. "Before September ends, we will get those apples."

"It's fine. They're just apples, KO."

"No, they're not," he said stubbornly. "They're part of Katy Keene's Most Fabulous Fall Ever, and I'm going to make sure you get to do *everything* on your list. Starting with hot apple cider. Let's get some from Starbucks and share it on the way uptown to Lacy's."

There were so many reasons I loved KO, and his dedication to apples was just one of them. I rose up to kiss him at the exact moment the police car idling at the curb next to us turned on its siren. Startled by the noise, KO turned his head, and my lips collided with his ear.

"Whoops." KO laughed. "I think you missed."

KO bent down to kiss me, and it was perfect, like always, but I couldn't shake the feeling I might have missed something else, too.

CHAPTER TWENTY-SIX
Jorge

"FORGET THE BIG HATS. FORGET the high-button shoes. Forget everything you know about *Hello, Dolly!*" Ethan Fox steepled his hands together, his voice grim.

I sat on the floor of another black box at the Private Theatre, a bigger one, surrounded by at least forty or fifty other actors. Maybe it *had* been a mistake to come back. I'd second-guessed myself on the train downtown, on the walk from the subway, and all the way in through the doors of the Private Theatre for the next round of callbacks.

But it was so hard to abandon the idea of this show, of working on Broadway, and even more, what this show might lead to. An Equity card, guaranteed. Maybe an agent. This could be the first show in a long, long career, and if I got this, I'd be able to skip past so much of the grunt work of trying to make it. I'd already have made it, before I even really started. And from what Ethan Fox had said at my last callback, it sounded like this part was mine to lose. Almost a sure thing.

Even just being able to perform in a show, night after night after night, would be such a gift. I hadn't been in anything since I graduated, and I already missed it so much. Maybe there was a way to take some of Ethan's notes while still performing in a way that felt true to me.

I took another look around. There were actors of all ages gathered in the theater. It was definitely more people than I'd expected. This must have been callbacks for all the principal roles, not the chorus, but at least it wasn't just other prospective Barnabys. I didn't see the hot guy from callbacks anywhere, though. Kevin Something. Guess he didn't make the cut. Well. One less thing to be distracted by.

"We will take this show apart, piece by piece, until only the core remains," Ethan continued. "The *truth*. The story of a matchmaker, a shopkeeper, and nothing less complicated than the human heart itself."

Um . . . okay. That seemed a little over-the-top, and usually I *loved* over-the-top, but this was over-the-top like when Jiggly Caliente channeled a baked potato on the *Drag Race* mainstage. I snuck a peek at the guy next to me, trying to sense his reaction, but he looked utterly rapt. I knew Ethan Fox was supposed to be a genius, and he was a genius who was rooting for *me*, so I should give his vision a chance—even if I wasn't exactly feeling it yet.

"Please. Join me." Ethan Fox closed his eyes, so I did, too. "Yonkers. The 1890s. Not the twee setting we've been led to believe. A mere stone's throw away from a city drawing immigrants by the thousands, brushing up against an increasingly xenophobic populace demanding immigration restriction. A bastion of industrial expansion revolutionizing itself too rapidly for control. A cesspool teeming with disease, death, and despair. A time of intense social, economic, and political anxiety. A time of intense *anxiety*, full stop."

I was having intense anxiety, full stop. I cracked an eye open. I felt like I was being inducted into a cult. Suddenly, the floor was feeling awfully cold against my legs, exposed in my lucky green audition shorts. I dug around in my dance bag until I pulled out my sweatpants and started to shimmy them up my legs. The boomer in front of me turned around to glare. Calm down, chica. That wasn't noisy. If she wanted noisy, I could get noisy.

"And this city, this is where our characters venture into. And this space is where our audience enters into. Open your eyes. See this with me." Ethan Fox steepled his hands together again, took a deep breath, and began. "The theater is no longer a stage. Not as we know it. There will be dirt under our feet, under the audience's feet, dirt serving as our stage. Inevitably, it will be tracked through the space, leaving its indelible mark on all of us here, just as the city grime of more than a century ago would have been impossible to shake."

This sounded like Ma's worst nightmare. If I got cast, she'd probably roll up to opening night in a full hazmat suit.

"And the walls?" Ethan stretched his arm. "Lined with the goods of Horace Vandergelder's feed and grain store. What's that sound?" He cupped a hand to his ear. "It's not just the all-new orchestrations, played only on banjo and the washboard. It's also the slow drip of grain and seed falling, an inexorable drip, drip, drip as time passes. And what's the audience sitting on? Chairs? Please. Nothing so pedestrian. They'll be sitting on more sacks of grain, each with a small hole, slowly dripping out their contents, just like the sacks on the walls, symbolizing the depletion of resources in the already taxed economy of America's largest city."

If I paid $250 for a Broadway ticket to find out I was sitting on a grain sack with a hole in it, I would have *words* for the usher.

"This is a visceral *Hello, Dolly!* A *Dolly* you can feel. A *Dolly* you can *smell*. And what is that smell, you ask?" Ethan Fox tapped the side of his nose. "That's stew. Bubbling away. A literal melting pot, blending the flavors from the European immigrants pouring into an already teeming city."

Was this stew a metaphor? Or was he talking *actual* stew?

"And at intermission, the audience will be able to really eat the stew, ladled into tin bowls by members of the cast." Real stew it was. Okay, then. "They'll be able to *taste* the gristle, contending with the marrow of the American experience."

Ooh, girl. If I wanted to taste the gristle, I'd just eat more of Joaquin's meat castoffs from work.

"And as for you?" Ethan continued. "The cast? You'll be stripped down to your raw essence, performing in deconstructed nineteenth-century undergarments." Okay, that I could get behind. I'd look cute in a corset. "The choreography will be dangerous and sensual. The crowd scenes will be violent and brutal. That parade passing by? It's a bloodbath, a riot caused by the pushing and shoving of the crowd, innocent bystanders trampled underfoot. Anyone could get stabbed at any moment."

Was Ethan Fox going to stab us?! The stew was real. How did we know the knives wouldn't be???

"And today, I hope you'll all feel the *stab* of inspiration." The room exploded into more laughter than that joke deserved. The thirstiness was at an all-time high here. "Although this *Hello, Dolly!* shall be built upon the scaffold of my vision, as those of you who have worked with me before know, I foster an environment of collaboration. These characters and this production will be *your* creations as well." Now, that sounded more appealing. Maybe all I needed to do was show these fools that I was the Barnaby they were *really* looking for, not some dude bro dancer type. I mean, *I* wouldn't have to sit on a grain sack. I could ladle some stew if the man needed me to ladle some stew. For an Equity card? I'd ladle all the stew he wanted. "So we'll begin the collaboration today, in callbacks. We'll be rotating through dancing, singing, and reading sides, and you'll all be participating or observing throughout the process. Use your fellow actors. They are your greatest resource."

Oh snap. I'd auditioned for a show like this once before, when my high school drama teacher had been feeling extra-creative or something. We'd all had to sit around in a circle and watch as, one by one, each person did a Shakespeare monologue. Which meant you never really got to relax, because you had to have your best "I'm invested and listening" face on the whole time. Ugh.

The monitor from the last round of callbacks stepped up with her clipboard, reading our names off a list and splitting us up into groups. Now, this was definitely by character. I stood in a group of fit guys with dancer bodies, ages eighteen to thirty-five. We must have been all the Barnabys and Corneliuses. The choreographer—instantly recognizable because he was the only person at the table in dance pants, plus I recognized him from the first dance call—led us down the hall to a dance studio.

I watched carefully as the choreographer broke down the combo. It reminded me of the *Newsies* routine we'd done at BDC—definitely wasn't the Gower Champion dance from the original Broadway production of *Hello, Dolly!* or the Michael Kidd one from the Barbra Streisand movie. I'd watched some of both on YouTube just in case. Luckily, all these kicks and jumps were exactly my jam.

After the first run, the choreographer moved me to the front row. But I didn't even need that validation to know I was slaying it.

With each run through the combo, my doubts about the show faded away. Maybe it was being surrounded by so many other people who wanted it, but I found myself wanting this gig, too. Desperately. I lost myself in the dance, in the music, forgetting about all that crap they'd said at my first callback and focusing only on keeping my turns tight and my arms crisp. I was dancing like putting on my Sunday clothes was the best thing that had ever happened to me. I was *living* for these Sunday clothes.

After one last run, we waited around awkwardly while a few more casting people, including Ethan Fox, came in to deliberate with the choreographer. After a couple minutes, they read out a list of people who could go home. The guy next to me burst into tears. But they didn't read my name. Trying to be respectful of the crying guy's emotional process, I held myself back from fist-pumping. Barely.

"Lopez, right?" The choreographer called me over before we left for the next room. I was half panicking that he'd decided to cut me, too, and half giddy that maybe he'd decided to cast me on the spot. "You're the one who dances with Jason, right?"

"Yeah. I mean, I take his classes."

"I can tell. Good stuff out there."

Lucky green audition shorts, you'd done it again! He

hadn't talked to anyone else. As I hustled out of the room, following the rest of the Barnabys and Corneliuses, I knew as long as everything else went well, the part was mine.

That Equity card was so close I could taste it.

Up next, in a room with a piano, we sang "Put On Your Sunday Clothes." My extreme hype about the Sunday clothes continued. We sang alone, and in pairs of Barnabys and Corneliuses, to make sure we could nail the harmony. While I was singing, Ethan Fox came into the room to listen, and smiled at me.

This part was mine. It was *so* mine, and these other Barnabys would have to rip it out of my cold, dead, gorgeous hands if they wanted it.

Finally, we walked down the hall to the last room, to read sides. This may have been what tripped me up last time, but this would be different. I knew it. I'd been Barnaby for hours. At this point, I *was* Barnaby. I wanted to see that whale just like he did. I wanted to go to New York. I wanted to see the world outside of Yonkers. I'd even deliberate on the influx of immigrants in the late nineteenth century, if Ethan Fox wanted me to!

Listen. Just because I didn't sweat beef and beer didn't mean I wasn't masculine. I was masculine in my own way, and the fact that I had the full, gorgeous lips of a young Sophia Loren didn't change that. And he wanted tough? I knew all about tough. You didn't wear blue mascara to an eighth-grade dance if you weren't tough. I'd just be tough like *me*. Grounded. Strong *because* I was soft. If Ethan Fox meant what he said about collaborating, he'd see what I could bring to the table, and realize it was exactly what he needed. Maybe he'd listened, really listened, to what I'd said at callbacks, and was ready to see me work with fresh eyes.

I shook hands with my scene partner, smiled, and began reading, ready to make my dreams come true.

CHAPTER TWENTY-SEVEN
Pepper

@PepperSmith ✅

Reassuring to know that in an increasingly corporate New York, there are still some places that thrum with authenticity.

@PepperSmith ✅

@TinysJazzClub is a true New York icon; old school in the best possible way

@PepperSmith ✅

What is jazz, anyway, if not the ideal soundtrack for our modern age?

@PepperSmith ✅

Life *is* improvisation

@PepperSmith ✓

In music and in life, one must break the rules in order to truly *create*

@PepperSmith ✓

Jazz legend @MylesMcCoyJazz is playing THE @TinysJazzClub in an unscheduled tour stop tonight; very old school *real* music

> **@TinysJazzClub**
>
> Can we put you on the list, @PepperSmith? We'd love to have you in the house at the show tonight!

> **@PepperSmith** ✓
>
> @TinysJazzClub Don't be thirsty, darling; I'll be there if I can be there.

CHAPTER TWENTY-EIGHT
Josie

MY FABULOUS NEW YORK ADVENTURE began in an underground garage called Big Apple Parking on West Eleventh Street. Decidedly not so fabulous. But once Pauly handed over the keys to the van to a valet who miraculously backed it into a teeny space between two other cars, Dad, Pauly, and I climbed up the stairs and emerged onto a street lined with redbrick buildings boasting tall windows, colorful doors, and wrought-iron fire escapes. It looked like a movie set. I had thought, when I finally made it to New York, I'd be disappointed, like it could never compare to what I'd dreamed.

But this was even better.

"Welcome to the West Village, Josie." Dad clapped a hand on my shoulder. "Let's go check in at Tiny's, then you can go explore a little."

"Seriously?" I was so shocked; Dad's sudden burst of

let's-give-Josie-her-freedom had stopped me in my tracks. I had to jog a bit to catch up with Dad and Pauly.

"Seriously. But no heading uptown to see the skyscrapers or Empire State Building or Fifth Avenue—"

"What about the Apollo? Minton's?" My heart sank, thinking about all the legendary music venues in Harlem I'd hoped to see.

"No way. You don't have time to go up to Harlem. But I love where your head's at." Dad grinned. "You're definitely my kid."

This was new. Usually I felt like Dad was pointing out all the ways we were different. Like his commitment to jazz versus the pop music I loved that he held in disdain. Or his professionalism versus what he saw as my lack of focus. It felt nice to be acknowledged like this, to know that he saw music as the thread that bound us together. Because whatever other issues I had with Dad, I never doubted for a moment that the man lived and breathed for his music.

"It'll be good to get back to Tiny's. Too bad Boone couldn't join us in New York and get a real feel for the Myles McCoy show before he joins the tour," Dad said.

Boone would be meeting us in Virginia Beach once we left New York, and then continuing on with the Myles McCoy show as we traveled farther south. I was still completely shocked that it was happening.

"He saw us in Toledo," I pointed out.

"Everybody sounds better at Tiny's, Josie." Pauly winked. "You'll see."

"That kid can sing," Dad admitted, clearly still thinking about Boone. "At the end of the day, all that really matters is talent. And he's got it."

I agreed. I mean, country music wasn't my thing, either, but the truth was undeniable: Boone Wyant had *a voice*. Even thinking about hearing him sing in Pittsburgh sent shivers up my spine.

"Do you think it'll help fill some of those empty seats?" I asked Pauly in an undertone as Dad checked something on his phone.

"Adding Boone? Oh yeah. It made financial sense," Pauly said. "We've been having some trouble filling venues on the later tour dates. Diversifying the genre of music in the show, especially with someone who's pretty well-known regionally, made sense."

If Dad's jazz shows were suddenly overrun with Boone Wyant superfans in denim cutoffs, I would die laughing.

We passed a pizza joint, a bar called Molly's Crisis—*huh, weird name for a bar*—a comedy club, and then, there it was. A small black awning with a trumpet on it proclaimed that we'd arrived at Tiny's. Dad pushed the black door set in the redbrick building, opening up to a set of stairs leading down to the basement.

For such an icon of jazz, it was, indeed, tiny. The ceiling was low, and the space was broken up by support beams. The stage was at the back of the club against a wall of exposed brick that had been painted black. It was really only a platform that had barely been raised a couple inches, not even a stage.

But I loved it immediately. It wasn't as glamorously decorated as Veronica had done up La Bonne Nuit, but being back in a basement dedicated to music felt like coming home. The quiet darkness of the stage enveloped me like a hug.

"Myles McCoy!" An older Black woman with a shaved head appeared behind the bar, her tassel earrings swinging as she set a crate of clean glasses down. "It is so good to see your ugly mug back at Tiny's." She crossed over to Dad and enveloped him in a hug. "When are you going to move to the city, huh? Can I get you off the road?"

"Not yet, Shirley." Dad hugged her back. "I've still got a few good miles left in me."

"Hmm. I doubt the plebes in Peoria appreciate you the way I do. Good to see ya, Pauly." She moved onto Pauly and gave him a hug, too, clapping him on the back. "You taking good care of our boy?"

"The best," he replied.

"And this must be Josie." She stood in front of me. "I'm Shirley, this is my jazz club, and you're gorgeous. Well, Josie, if you sing like you look, you'll be a star in no time, sweetheart."

"That's the plan."

"Good. I like a girl with ambition." She smiled at me. "And with great taste in earrings."

"Why, thank you." I touched my favorite pair of hoops, happy I'd pushed my hair back with a slim silver headband to show them off a bit. The slight pressure from the headband made me feel almost like I was wearing my old Pussycat ears. With my ears on, I'd always felt invincible.

Or maybe that was just because I'd had Val and Melody at my side.

I know the fact that I exerted a lot of creative control caused tension with the Pussycats, but I was missing those days. Touring with Dad, I had literally *zero* control. Over anything.

"You want to open for your dad tonight?" Shirley asked. "As a solo act?"

Huh? *Seriously?!* Dad had never asked me to open for him. In fact, before we'd even left Riverdale, he had been pretty clear that it would *never* happen. He was the star. I was support staff. And if I even so much as *hinted* that I was daring to do anything remotely diva-ish, like, oh, you know, sing a song that *I* had chosen, I could find some other jazz musician to tour with.

Which seemed like a pretty unlikely prospect.

"Who? Me?" I stuttered, dying to know what was playing across my dad's face but afraid to look.

"I'm not asking Pauly."

"Hey, easy, Shirl, I've been working on my juggling." I had no idea whether or not Pauly was joking or not. "I'm almost ready to hit the big time."

"You haven't even heard me sing." Dad hadn't shut the

185

idea down. I was practically cringing, waiting for him to nix the whole thing, but he hadn't yet.

"Then let's hear you sing."

Shirley walked over to the stage and took a seat at the black upright piano pushed against one wall. I followed her, stepping onto the stage and adjusting the microphone down to the right height. Even without the stage lights on, and with the bar flooded by daytime fluorescents, there was still magic in stepping in front of a microphone. Pauly had taken a seat at a table in the front row, smiling expectantly. Dad remained standing, his face inscrutable.

"Do you know 'Remember Me'?" I asked. If I wanted to be the next Diana Ross, I might as well be the next Diana Ross. "By Diana Ross?"

"Do I know it." She chuckled. "Honey, I've lived it."

The opening notes played. I closed my eyes and took a deep breath.

"Bye baby," I crooned into the microphone. "See you around."

The bar was utterly silent except for me and Shirley at the piano. I blocked out the fact that Dad was listening and just sang the song I loved. When I finished, the bar remained silent.

"Well, Myles, looks like you've got yourself an opener," Shirley said eventually. "That was really something, Josie," she added, with feeling.

"Looks like I do." Dad wasn't smiling, exactly, but I thought the corners of his mouth turned up a little. "Five songs. And please don't sing anything that will make people leave."

"Thanks, Dad." I rolled my eyes. "Love the vote of confidence."

"Write your set list down for me, baby," Shirley instructed. "There's pen and paper behind the bar. We'll have the house band back you up. Don't worry about going too obscure, either. They know *everything.*"

Wow. My very own solo show, in New York City! Sure, it was only five songs, and I was opening for Dad, but still! Five songs that I could choose! I was so excited to be able to sing exactly what I wanted to.

And before that, I had an afternoon free. In a place that was a lot more interesting than a Comfort Motel. Leaving Dad, Pauly, and Shirley at Tiny's, set list complete behind the bar, I practically skipped up the stairs and onto the sidewalk.

I grabbed a slice of pizza that only cost ninety-nine cents and was absolutely delicious. I ate it on the sidewalk, watching the taxis careen down the street. I probably could have been doing something more exciting with my one day in New York, but all I really wanted to do was wander. I strolled the aisles at a record store, browsed the racks at a few small boutiques, and ate an extremely pastel cupcake, sitting on the stoop of a brownstone that probably cost more than most of the housing stock in Riverdale combined. But maybe this was the magic of New York. I wasn't doing anything, but just by being here, surrounded by the people and the energy, I *felt* like I was doing something.

I felt like *I* was someone.

I made it back to Tiny's just before call time. Touching up my makeup in the minuscule dressing room, I could hear the jazz club filling up, little snippets of laughter and conversation floating back to me. Shirley herself came backstage to let me know it was five minutes to places.

I waited backstage, peeping out from behind the curtain at the packed house. Shirley walked out to introduce me, and I walked confidently onstage, soaking up the applause.

"Hello, New York City!" I said, adjusting the microphone.

And the cheers that answered me sounded like coming home.

CHAPTER TWENTY-NINE
Katy

THIS TIME, I DIDN'T HAVE a buddy to ride up the elevator with. I was on my own.

Probably because I was ridiculously early.

The doors to the sixth floor opened up and I fled down the hall, sighing with relief that my garment bag was still on one of the rolling racks. And it looked like everyone else's garment bags were there, too, thank goodness. Yesterday at Lacy's, I'd been so in my own head about the modeling thing, I hadn't even noticed what everybody else had done with their clothes.

I still wasn't, you know, *thrilled* about making my runway debut, but I was feeling better about it, at least. As silly as it had been, walking the makeshift runway with Jorge at Molly's Crisis had helped. As had watching all the reality TV he'd assigned me as homework, although that was mostly because it was relaxing, not so much because it was instructional. And, of course, taking the train uptown with KO had helped tremendously. I always felt calmer with him by my side. Maybe KO was right, and it would all be no big deal.

One by one, the other designers arrived. There were six of us total. I exchanged friendly waves with Deja before she shrugged off her coat, revealing a well-tailored blouse with a pussycat bow that was literally printed with cats. I was completely obsessed with her whole vibe. She knew what she liked, and she just *went for it*.

Last, but certainly not least, Rex London swept through the doors, Andy and his ever-present clipboard at his side. Today, Rex wore a suit but no tie, his floral-printed shirt contrasting in a coordinated way with his gingham pocket square in the same color story. Maybe I needed to start mixing patterns more confidently, because I was loving it on him.

"So, so sorry about cutting things short yesterday," Rex apologized. "Here's a tip, baby designers: Never go into television. It's not worth the hassle!"

We all nodded, like we were currently fielding multiple offers from television networks. Although, actually, what did I know? Maybe the others were. I remembered what Andy had said about everyone else's presence on social media and felt a few pinpricks of inadequacy. I did my very best to squash them. Jorge had insisted that what separated a good model from a bad one was confidence. All I had to do was *pretend* I knew what I was doing.

"Fake it 'til you make it *works*, Katy-girl," he'd said. "Like that time I said I had tap experience when I auditioned to play Michael in *A Chorus Line*. Did I? Nope. But I just said, 'I can do that,' and I did it. And did I have tap experience by the end of the run? You bet your tiny lil booty I did."

"I can do that," I whispered to myself. All I had to do was find a point, focus on it, and walk. "I can do that."

I'd also watched an old YouTube clip from *A Chorus Line* last night. You know, for motivation. Although I'd mostly ended up inspired by the '80s leotards. They were kind of epic.

"So. Today." Rex London clapped his hands. "One by one, you'll put on your garments, I'll give you some last-minute critiques, and then we'll block out the show, walking order, all that good stuff. For the actual show, we'll be walking downstairs, in the perfume hall, but we'll just mock through it up here for now."

We'd be walking in the perfume hall?! How cool! I couldn't believe my first fashion show was taking place in the main hall of Lacy's, a place that had meant so much to me for my whole life.

I just wished someone *else* could walk for me. Like, an actual model. Someone who knew how to make my clothes look good. I couldn't mess this up. If I tripped in Lacy's, I'd be too humiliated to come back, and that was an unimaginable fate.

Well. First things first. I had to get through this fitting

before I worried about walking. Rex London still hadn't seen my dress. I was hoping it was better than I'd remembered. I'd gotten so in my head about it, I honestly had no idea whether it was good or bad anymore.

I took a seat next to Deja as Rex called us up one by one. With each design he looked at, I got more and more nervous. To me, the suits and dresses and jumpsuits I saw all looked perfect, so professional, but Rex always found something to critique. He wasn't mean, necessarily, but he didn't hold back, either. I had to consciously stop myself from jiggling my legs with anxiety.

Deja was up there now, modeling what looked like a flight suit but made out of bright emerald silk printed with leopards and jungle flowers. The tailoring at the nipped-in waist was exquisite. And when she just casually mentioned that she'd screen printed the design herself, I almost fell off my chair. Everyone here was seriously good. Did I have what it took to measure up?

"Katy Keene!" Rex called. "Our final designer. I'm so eager to see what you have for us!"

"Extremely eager!" Andy said, clapping.

I brought my garment bag into the changing area set up in one corner of the room behind a folding screen and started getting undressed.

"I understand, of course, that you haven't had as much time as the rest of the designers," Rex called as I finished changing, zipping up my dress with shaking fingers. The nerves were out in full force, and my best efforts to channel Jorge's confidence were failing me. "And that you haven't had the benefit of receiving any input from me on your design. So just know that I do have that in mind . . ."

As I rounded the corner, now dressed in my look for the fashion show, Rex trailed off mid-sentence. And from the look on his face, I got the feeling he wasn't speechless with wonder.

At least, not the good kind of wonder.

"Here it is!" I did an awkward set of ta-da hands and stood on the little raised platform in front of the three-way mirror. I was trying my very best to fake it, honestly, but I got the feeling I couldn't fake my way out of this one. This wasn't a tap dance audition for a high school production of *A Chorus Line*. This was just me, in a dress, standing alone in a brightly lit room at Lacy's. I may have been fully clothed, but I'd never felt so exposed. Rex London crossed his arms and frowned at me.

"And what . . . is . . . *it*, exactly?" Rex asked.

Well, that wasn't the question I wanted to hear.

"It's, um, a dress?" I plucked nervously at a phantom thread at my wrist.

"Interesting. Is it? I see a high neckline with a floral detail. I see a chiffon bell sleeve. I see a plaid vest. I see a pleated A-line skirt. I see a collection of random elements that do not go together in the slightest which are, granted, reasonably well-constructed, but I do not see *a dress*."

I exhaled slowly, trying with everything I had to fight the prickle of tears at my eyes and the burning in the back of my throat. I had known, coming into today, that this probably wasn't going to be good.

But it was so, so much worse than I'd feared. Standing under the soft glow of the store's most flattering lighting, I could see, for the first time, how truly bad this dress was. There was a case to be made that a garment consisting of seemingly incongruous elements had always been a way to move the fashion needle forward—just look at the prints that came out of the '60s, or even the pattern mixing that Rex was so fond of—but this dress wasn't worth defending. It wasn't intentionally incongruous. It wasn't intentionally *anything*.

And the worst part? It wasn't *me* at all. Looking at myself in the mirror, I felt like I was wearing something that had been made by a stranger.

I braced myself for the gossipy whispers of the other designers, but instead, the room was absolutely silent, which was somehow even more humiliating. Even with the plush carpeting, I was confident you could easily have heard a pin drop.

"Tell me, Katy Keene. Has Veronica Lodge actually *seen* anything you've designed?" Rex asked. "Because I know Veronica, and she is an absolute paragon of style who wouldn't be caught dead in an atrocity like this."

"No," I whispered, looking down, afraid to make eye contact with Rex, or to see what was written on the other designers' faces. Probably pity at best, and disdain at the worst. "I mean, yes, she's seen things I've made, but she wouldn't wear this dress."

"I honestly cannot imagine a single person who would. Can you step off the dais, please?" Closing his eyes, he pinched the bridge of his nose. "Seeing this monstrosity reflected in the three-fold in the mirror is triggering a migraine."

"Good thing we decided to go paperless." Andy pulled a packet of aspirin out of his pants pocket. Rex waved him away. "I can easily remove Miss Keene from all the literature before the show. In fact, I can do it right now." He pulled his phone out of another pants pocket.

"No, no." Rex sank into a chair, his elbow resting delicately on the arm as he looked at me like I was the worst thing to happen to fashion since low-rise jeans. "I'd rather not make a change now and get the bloggerati talking. Better we just don't include her on the day of. No one will notice. Unless . . ." One eyebrow arched up. "Unless you think you can salvage this?"

"*Salvage* this? Are we looking at the same random collection of half-baked trends?" Andy whispered, wincing, like he didn't want me to hear him.

"Perhaps Miss Keene is one of those creative types who works best under pressure."

"I can salvage it." Could I? Mom would have known exactly what elements to keep and what to toss, and how to turn it into something special. Me? I had no idea. But I couldn't let my big chance slip through my fingers without at least trying one more time.

"We don't lose anything by letting her try." Rex shrugged. "Show up at Lacy's an hour before call time for the fashion show. If it's good, you walk. If it's not, I never want to hear the name 'Katy Keene' again as long as I live. Understood?"

"Understood." I nodded. "I can fix it. I promise. Thank you for giving me another chance. I know I probably don't deserve it."

"Probably not," he mused, "but the concept of whether or not one 'deserves' something is always so unappealing to me. Who deserves anything, really?" I nodded like I understood what he was saying, but I didn't, really. My brain was too busy melting with shame to focus on his meditation on the nature of what humanity does or doesn't deserve. "I'd change before leaving, if I were you," he said. "You wouldn't want to scare the customers."

Right. Summarily dismissed, I vanished behind the screen to change back into my street clothes. As Rex began blocking the show, arranging the designers in the order they were going to walk in, the room returned to its normal level of volume.

I held it together as I stuffed my horrible dress back in the garment bag, carried it onto the elevator, and fled through the perfume hall and out the doors, but the second I hit the sidewalk, the tears started flowing freely. My big chance, and I'd ruined it. What a complete and utter disaster. I took a seat on a stone planter on the sidewalk, perching on the edge, the plants within long gone for the summer and yet to be replaced by tiny Christmas trees. Looking up at Lacy's, at the beautiful window display with the trailing scarves, I couldn't believe it had been so recently that I'd stood here with KO in front of this exact same window, so full of optimism for the best fall ever.

Some fall this was shaping up to be. Did I even have what it took to be a professional designer? If this was what happened to me the first time I had to design under pressure, I should probably just give up. If I was lucky, that man at Howie's Hoagies would still have the job available. Right now, "sandwich" seemed like the only career opportunity I was fit for.

Sighing, I pulled out my phone. My finger hovered over the contacts, wondering if I should call KO for sympathy, or Jorge for a pep talk, but then I realized I didn't want to talk to either one of them. Thinking about recounting how badly I'd failed made me flood with shame all over again. Telling them would make it more real somehow.

There was only one person I wanted to talk to, and she wasn't here anymore.

What I wouldn't give for one more minute with Mom.

No wonder I was flailing. This was the first thing I'd tried to design since Mom died. Without her to bounce my ideas off of, or offer suggestions on my sketches, or help me tackle a particularly tricky pleat, designing any-thing felt impossible. I needed her, not just for this dress, but for everything. She'd been right by my side—from the first sloppy pillowcase I sewed all the way through to the elaborate construction of my prom dress. By then, she was too weak to sit at the sewing machine, but her eye was sharp as ever. She made me the designer I was—and she was the designer I wanted to be.

Could I do this without her?

I wasn't sure. But I knew she'd want me to *try*.

Wiping my face on the back of my sleeve, too upset to care about the trails of mascara staining the red sleeves of my coat, I pushed myself up off the planter. I didn't have Mom anymore, but I did have one piece of her she'd left behind. The place I turned to, whenever I needed things to make sense. Stuffing my garment bag under my arm, I turned decidedly toward the stairs to the subway, ready to head downtown.

I needed to get back to my sewing machine.

CHAPTER THIRTY
Jorge

I PINCHED MY IMAGINARY BOWLER hat between my thumb and index finger and fanned out the rest of my hand. Nothing like a little Fosse to distract a guy from the endless waiting to find out if his life was going to change.

"Natalie! Those aren't Fosse fingers!" Jason Bravard called, the studio at Broadway Dance Center filled with dozens of Advanced Musical Theatre students doing their very best Fosse moves across the floor. "And Jorge. Are you even *trying* to point your toes on the kick? Doesn't matter how high it is if your feet are ugly!"

Point. Right. Fosse. Focus.

I'd kept my ringer on my phone on loud, with the volume all the way up. Obnoxious, but I wasn't going to risk missing a call from the *Hello, Dolly!* team. Every once in a while, I'd snuck a glance over at my bag, but so far, it was depressingly silent. If your phone rang during class, it *better* be because you'd booked a gig, otherwise, the wrath of Jason Bravard was swift and unforgiving.

I hit the final pose, elbows in, arms flat, fingers spread wide.

"And one more time!" Jason called. Barely suppressed groans reverberated through the room. I wiped the sweat off my forehead with the edge of my crop top and got back into position for the top of the number.

One last run later, complete with very pointed toes on the kicks, we were dismissed. Following the rest of the class, I shuffled over to the edge of the room, crouching down to pull my water bottle out of my dance bag. And at that exact moment, sweaty and mid-gulp, my phone rang. Pulse racing, I dug through my bag until I pulled it out from under a cropped hoodie. I looked at the screen—a number I didn't recognize with a New York area code. Que mierda. It was either a telemarketer, or it was *the* call. Vibrating with anxiety, still crouched over my dance bag, I answered the phone.

"Hello?"

"Hi there," an unfamiliar woman's voice said. "Is this Jorge Lopez?"

"Yes!" I squealed. "Um, yeah. I mean, yes," I said, more sedately, like someone who was used to getting calls from Broadway casting offices all the time. "Yes, this is he."

"Great. Well, we just wanted to let you know that, unfortunately, we've gone in another direction."

"You've—I'm sorry, what?" What was happening? I had been so sure I'd crushed it. They'd laughed at all the funny lines when I'd read, without a single note about me being "too soft" or too anything else. They'd kept me in the room for hours, rotating out different Corneliuses as I read scene after scene, like they were testing who played best against *me*. Like I was already cast! And now, they were *calling* me to tell me I *didn't* get it? How was this possible? Anytime I hadn't been cast in something before, I just never heard back from the theater, like they were ghosting me out of a relationship.

"At the end of the day, for Barnaby, Ethan was just looking for someone with a little more . . . edge."

"Yes, a character whose catchphrase is 'holy cabooses!' is definitely known for his edge."

It just slipped out. I hadn't meant to be so sarcastic. Even though I was pissed, I thought I knew better than to be so flip with a casting person, potentially burning a bridge. Stupid. I bit my tongue as the pause on the other end of the line stretched on into infinity. During that pause, I died, was reincarnated as myself, lived another eighteen years, and came back to wait on the phone.

"Thank you for your time," she said flatly, then hung up.

I didn't get it. Everything I thought could come from this show: my Equity card, an agent, a real job on Broadway, gone. In a ninety-second phone call. I buried my head in my hands, squeezing my eyes shut.

"Guessing that wasn't the call you wanted." I looked up to see Jason Bravard standing above me, a sympathetic smile on his face. "*Hello, Dolly!*?"

"Yeah." Avoiding eye contact, I pulled my jacket out of my bag and shrugged it on. "But, you know. There'll be other shows."

That wasn't how I felt. It felt like my world was ending. But sometimes I did my best acting offstage. Like right now, when I was trying to save face in front of my scary-talented and sometimes just plain scary dance teacher, who had more than enough edge. I had a feeling that Jason Bravard had never been told he was "too soft" for anything. Except maybe the Navy SEALs, although, honestly, he probably could make the cut for that, too. I'd like to see a Navy SEAL attempt a fan kick.

"Yes. There will be." I rose to my feet, still trying to avoid Jason's piercing stare. "I know this isn't what you want to hear right now, but you're young, Jorge. You're really young. You've got time. So much time. This is only your beginning."

"Thanks." Jason being nice to me was just making me even more upset. I felt more comfortable around him when he was critiquing me for not pointing my toes enough. Like, if he thought I was so sad that he had to be nice to me, I must have been *really* pathetic.

"Keep coming to class, okay?" he called as I walked out of the studio. "And keep auditioning!"

Ugh. The last thing I wanted to think about was another audition. I wanted sweatpants and Cheetos and people crying their fake eyelashes off on some train wreck of a reality TV show. I wanted nothing that had to do with

Ethan Fox, or *Hello, Dolly!*, or Broadway, or any of it.

Well. There was someone walking past the windows in front of BDC who had nothing to do with any of those things. Unable to believe what I was seeing, I pushed open the doors to catch him.

"Dad?" I asked incredulously. He stopped in the middle of the sidewalk like he'd been caught doing something illegal. "What are you doing in Times Square?"

"I had a meeting on Ninth Avenue."

"Oh. Right." For a moment, I thought maybe he'd come to see me. Like we might grab a late lunch at Helen's Moonbeam Diner after dance class, like we used to when I was a little kid. Dad hated the singing waitresses there, but he always sucked it up because he knew how much I loved it. And because he liked their Blue Suede Burger.

"Well." Dad cleared his throat uncomfortably, his mustache twitching. "Shall we walk to the A train together?"

"Sure." He looked like he'd rather get ten root canals all at once. Why had I even run out after him? I should have just waited in the lobby at BDC until he was gone so I could have ridden uptown alone, listening to *Dear Evan Hansen* and crying in peace on the subway.

I didn't get the part. I couldn't believe I didn't get it.

"So." Against all the odds, there we were, walking south toward Forty-Second Street together. This was already the longest conversation we'd had in months. Maybe years. "Your mother tells me you've been auditioning for some big show."

Excellent. Exactly what I wanted to talk to my estranged father about. How I'd failed.

"Emphasis on *been* auditioning," I said. "I didn't get it."

I didn't get it. It reverberated in my head, over and over again. My big chance, and I'd screwed it up.

"Ah." The wind started to pick up. I pulled up my hood as Dad tucked his head down, sinking into his collar like a turtle dressed in business casual. "I'm sorry to hear that."

"It's fine."

It wasn't. None of this was fine. Not the fact that I didn't get the part, or that I was walking down the street with my father, talking to him like he was a total stranger, or the fact that we weren't saying any of the things that needed to be said. Was this what the rest of our lives would be like? Polite conversation, ignoring the fact that he didn't approve of my sexuality? Didn't approve of *me*? What would happen when I brought a guy home? Fell in love? Wanted to get married? At some point, my dad was going to have to choose: If he wanted me in his life, he needed *all* of me in his life.

Maybe coming home had been a mistake. This half-life with him, of pretending everything was fine, was too painful. But the idea of cutting my father out of my life completely was also more than I could bear. I needed more from him to move forward, but I didn't know how, or if, I was ever going to get it. Repairing our relationship couldn't be all on me. It was too much.

"You know what?" I said abruptly. "I left something at Broadway Dance Center. I need to go back."

"Jorge—"

"I have to go, okay?" I turned and ran up Eighth Avenue. I couldn't let him see me cry. I'd had enough "boys don't cry" from him to last me a lifetime.

"I'll see you at home, okay?" he called as I ran, disappearing into the crowd of tourists weaving their way toward Times Square.

Home.

It hadn't been home for a long, long time, and I was having a hard time seeing how it ever could be again.

CHAPTER THIRTY-ONE
Pepper

THE ELEVATOR DOORS SLID OPEN onto the rooftop bar, exposing an urban wonderland. The entire city was spread before us, the lights in a million windows twinkling. The rooftop itself looked like somewhere Alice could have tumbled into once she fell down the rabbit hole. There was greenery everywhere, strung with tiny fairy lights, and plush, comfortable couches set up in cozy conversation nooks. You weren't quite as high as you'd be at the top of the Empire State Building or at One World Trade Center, but you could still see plenty of the city, and the ambience more than made up for it.

"Welcome to the rooftop at 550, Miss Smith. We have it reserved for you for the entire evening," the elevator operator said. "I hope you enjoy your time here."

"I'm sure we will." I smiled at him. "Thank you so very much."

"Wow." Jules walked in front of me onto the roof, her long blonde hair tumbling down her back. In the brief time we'd been seeing each other, I'd learned she wasn't much for dressing up, but she looked absolutely stunning in plain black jeans and a leather jacket.

"I hope this makes up for the fact that I missed the jazz show at Tiny's," I said. I'd been planning to take Jules to the unplanned Myles McCoy show—I loved how old-school and, well, tiny, Tiny's was—but at the very last minute, Ethan Fox had texted, asking if I was available to take a meeting. Those theatre people and their odd hours. I had *thought* we were meeting to talk about him directing the play I'd written about how the Russian Revolution might have turned out differently if Anastasia had had access to Snapchat, but he'd only blathered on about the immigrant experience in Yonkers in the 1890s, in a futile attempt to get me to throw some money behind his production of *Hello, Dolly!* Please. If I wanted to eat stew while sitting on a grain sack, I didn't have to produce a musical in order to do it.

"Are you kidding? No offense to Myles McCoy, but there's no way he could compete with a view like this. Look!" She pointed excitedly. "The Empire State Building!"

"Well-spotted." Together, we walked toward the railing to look out at the city. The top of the Empire State Building was lit up blue, for reasons I didn't understand. Perhaps something to do with sports.

"I love this city," she whispered. "I love everything about it. It's so beautiful at night."

"You're beautiful."

I turned my head, and our lips met in a kiss. How lucky that our paths had randomly crossed in Central Park. Jules had been jogging by at a rather alarming clip, and I hadn't seen much besides a blur of blonde ponytail as I strolled at a more sedate pace, enjoying a macchiato and an almond croissant from Maison Kayser as I looked at the changing leaves. Luckily, Jules, the clever minx, had noticed *me* and taken a stretch break just a bit farther down the path. We had struck up a conversation and the rest, as they say, was history.

She'd certainly been making my time in New York even more enjoyable than I'd anticipated.

"This is amazing, Pepper," Jules whispered. She wrapped her arms around my waist and nestled her chin against my neck, standing right behind me as we looked out over the city. I could feel the wind blowing her hair against my cheek, tickling me slightly. "I can't believe I've lived in New York my whole life, and I've never seen anything like this."

"Don't be silly, darling, you live in *Queens*." I squeezed her arms. "That's hardly New York."

"Hey now." Jules removed her arms and stepped to the side, resting her elbows on the balcony. "I can put up with a lot, Pep," she teased, "but you do not disrespect Queens to my face. I don't want to fight you, but I will."

"Understood." I held up one arm conciliatorily, and she snuggled in. "Please don't fight me, darling. I don't have a death wish."

"You should come out to Astoria with me next weekend. See where I'm from. What it's really like."

"Mmm," I murmured noncommittally. The idea of trekking to an outer borough, even on Jules's well-defined arm, was thoroughly unappealing.

"We can get dinner at the Greek place down the street. It's unreal. Seriously. Like nothing you've ever had."

"I don't know; I split a grilled branzino with Alessandra Ambrosio in Mykonos once that transported me to another plane . . ."

"Pfft." Jules snorted. "Forget Mykonos. This'll be better. Plus they do amazing Greek fries, with feta and oregano sprinkled on top. And then we can get milk shakes at the Starlite. And maybe . . . maybe you could come over and meet my ma," she added hopefully. I could tell she was trying to be casual, but that this idea meant a lot to her. Which was making me nervous. I was not the "bring home and meet your ma" type. I'd started this thing with Jules thinking it would be just a fun, casual fling, but if we weren't on the same page, perhaps I'd need to end things sooner than I'd planned to. "I mean, just if we're in the neighborhood. No worries."

"That does sound charming, but I'm not sure I'll be able to make it," I said carefully. "I've committed to doing quite a bit of Fashion Week coverage for various media outlets, plus I've scheduled myself a brunch with Guy LaMontagne, only it's out at his summer home in Sag Harbor, so I'm not sure how long that will take . . ."

"Sure, sure. I totally get it." Jules's tone was breezy, but I was worried that her attitude toward whatever was between us was not. "Too soon for you to meet my ma, anyway. Forget it, Pep. I don't know what I was thinking." She smiled at me, the dimples in her cheeks adorable. "We've got plenty of time. Queens isn't going anywhere, right? It'll be waiting across the bridge whenever you're ready."

I certainly wasn't ready. And as I watched Jules look out over the city lights, gorgeous as she was, I didn't think I ever would be.

CHAPTER THIRTY-TWO
Josie

OBVIOUSLY, I WAS GLAD WE'D gotten to play Tiny's—the place was legendary for a reason, and it had felt so good to sing whatever I wanted to—but our quick detour to New York had wreaked havoc on the tour schedule. It was a six-and-half-hour drive from New York to Virginia Beach, and this was the longest stretch we'd done in one go so far. Now I understood why Pauly had carefully plotted out the tour so we usually didn't have to cross so many states at once.

I balled my sweatshirt up under my neck, trying to get comfortable. Maybe I should have bought one of those neck pillows they were selling at the last gas station we stopped at. After being stuck in the van for so long, my neck felt crunched, my back hurt, and I thought my leg muscles were starting to atrophy. No matter how much I tossed and turned, nothing felt right.

But eventually, finally, we got off the highway, thank the lord. Shockingly, we drove into the heart of Virginia Beach. When Pauly turned into the parking lot at the Beachfront Inn, which was literally on the beach, I wondered if he'd made a mistake.

"Are we staying here?" I was half-hopeful, half-afraid he was just gonna pop in real quick and ask for directions or something. "Seriously? Or is this just a pit stop on the way to the nearest Comfort Motel?"

"Yup. This is our stop. Got a great end-of-season deal. Thought it would be a nice way to welcome Boone to the tour," Pauly said.

I had to admit, spending the day on the beach with Boone Wyant sounded awfully appealing. I had known he was meeting up with us today, but I had no idea it would be in a situation that involved sun, sand, and potential shirtlessness.

Excited, I unbuckled my seat belt as soon as Pauly put the van in park, ran under the green awning and into the hotel, forgetting all about my suitcase. I needed a break from that van. I was already dreading getting back in it tomorrow to drive to Greenville, North Carolina. But for now, I'd try to focus on enjoying where I was. I crossed to the other end of the lobby, my nose pressed up against the glass. Unbelievable. There was a narrow green lawn, a strip of concrete boardwalk, and just beyond that, the beach. I couldn't believe how close we were. When Dad had said we were going to Virginia Beach, I didn't think

I'd actually *see* the beach. I'd assumed it'd be our regular view of highway lights and neon signs from fast-food joints. Honestly, I'd gotten so used to Comfort Motel lobbies that even seeing a different-colored throw pillow on the couches in the lobby was a thrill beyond belief.

"Lucky for you, it's still pretty warm out there!" the front desk clerk said cheerfully as I watched seagulls darting past. "Hope you brought your bikini. Is this your first time in Virginia Beach?"

"It is," I answered her.

"Well, welcome. You're gonna love it!"

I took a seat on a couch in the lobby while Dad and Pauly checked in. In the distance, through the big windows at the front of the hotel, I could see the waves rolling in along the beach. Maybe I'd even have time to find a bathing suit somewhere and go swimming! It did look pretty tempting. As Dad went to check out the coffee situation at the breakfast bar—I hoped he wasn't holding his breath for one of those fancy lattes he loved—Pauly joined me on the couch.

There was, however, one problem I'd spotted so far with Virginia Beach.

"Are there even going to be enough people here to come to a show?" I looked around the empty lobby, and then out through the windows to the empty boardwalk. "It's like a ghost town."

"Tourist season's over. It's no big surprise that the place has kind of emptied out." Pauly shrugged. "Not every gig can be three thousand seats at the Detroit Opera House. Or even a packed house at Tiny's."

"Right." I frowned, dreading playing to a half-empty house tonight.

"Don't worry, Josie." Pauly patted my shoulder. "The name Myles McCoy has never failed to put butts into seats before. And Boone Wyant should help, too. Bring in a younger demographic. That's why I wanted him to join the tour."

And like his name had summoned him, the lobby doors slid open, and Boone walked in. He only had a guitar case and a small duffel. Either he was the world's lightest packer, or he was keeping the rest of his stuff in his truck.

"Hey y'all." Boone greeted us with a wave.

"Welcome to the Myles McCoy tour, Boone." Pauly jumped to his feet and shook Boone's hand.

"Thanks, Pauly." Boone pulled Pauly and slapped him heartily on the back. "It's a real honor to be here."

"We're happy to have ya."

"Hello, Boone." Dad walked over to our corner of the lobby, a paper cup of coffee in his hands, breaking up the Pauly-Boone lovefest. "You've made it. Sound check is at five. Rooms aren't ready to check into yet, but you may leave your things with the front desk."

I'd seen Dad look more excited about a trip to the DMV. Dad had only said nice things about Boone's performance when it was just the three of us, but now that

Boone was here, you'd certainly never know it. Well, I knew firsthand how withholding Dad could be when it came to praise.

"Great, thank you, sir." Boone smiled, like Dad had just welcomed him with open arms instead of dispensed information with barely concealed disdain. "Josie, you wanna hit the beach?"

"Sure." It took every ounce of my self-control not to look at Dad to make sure he was okay with it. I was an almost-adult woman who didn't need to check with Daddy for every little thing, but it was hard not to. Both as my dad, and as the guy who was running the show.

Boone left his bag and guitar at the front desk, and we walked through the sliding glass doors that opened onto the beach. Crossing the concrete boardwalk, we descended a small flight of stairs onto the sand. The beach stretched out seemingly for miles in either direction, the ocean in front of us a limitless expanse of blue. We certainly had nothing like this back home. No offense to Riverdale, but Sweetwater River just couldn't compare.

I tried to tuck some flyaway curls behind my ears and failed. It may have been unseasonably warm, but it was windier down here, and I could definitely feel it.

"Look at that view." Boone whistled. "It's got nothing on the Great Smoky Mountains, but it's not half-bad."

"It always comes back to Tennessee with you," I teased.

"How about you come back to Tennessee with me?" he asked.

"Sure. When the tour runs through Nashville. I'll be there."

"Not just on tour. You should move there," Boone said.

"Move there?" I raised an eyebrow. "What would I do in Nashville?"

"Make connections. Get started as a solo artist."

The idea of branching out on my own, especially after *finally* getting a taste of my own show at Tiny's, was definitely appealing. But Nashville?

"I don't know anybody there."

"You know me." He grinned. "I could introduce you to some people. Producers and managers and bookers for all the best venues. I could even get you a day job at the Heartless Café. Just until you make it big, of course."

"Of course." Could Nashville really be the place for me? Having a leg up with some of Boone's connections definitely couldn't hurt . . .

"I can't wait to show you my city." He tucked one of my windblown curls behind my ear, but it immediately sprang free again. Slowly, like he was worried he might spook me, his hand moved from behind my ear to the side of my face. He cupped my cheek, tilted up my chin, and before the next wave rolled in, we were kissing.

He kissed like he sang.

I pushed gently against his chest, the slight pressure from my hands enough that he broke the kiss immediately.

"Boone." I shook my head, my curls bouncing in and

out of my peripheral vision. "Wait a minute. What are we doing?"

"Kissing." He grinned. "And doing a pretty good job of it, too, if I do say so myself."

"Be serious." I pushed against his chest again. Someone had clearly been hitting the hotel gym while on tour. "What is this?" I gestured in the space between the two of us. "Like, what could this even be?"

"Well, we don't know what it is yet. That's where the kissing comes in. It's a great way to figure things out."

He closed his eyes again, but I stopped him before his lips met mine.

"Kissing never figured anything out," I said. "It just complicates things. And the last thing I need while I'm getting my career started is complications." Sighing, he stuck his hands into the pockets of his jeans. "I know we're in the same place right now, but that'll just be for a couple of tour dates. Then we'll be off in different directions, and realistically, we'll probably never see each other again."

"Maybe not. Maybe we'll both be in Nashville. So why not see where it goes?" he asked. "For now?"

"I've done that before. I've even done the short-term fling with an expiration date thing," I said, thinking about Sweet Pea. "These things are never as clean as you think they'll be."

"Forget clean. I think it'd be an awful lot of fun to get messy with you, Josie McCoy."

That didn't sound half-bad. It would be so easy to close

my eyes, wind my arms around his neck, and kiss him again. I could see the rest of the tour playing out in front of me. The two of us laughing as we flew down the highway in his pickup truck, sharing snacks and fighting over what station to listen to on the radio. Singing together, in front of a packed house, but feeling like we were the only two people in the room. Stealing kisses backstage and holding hands in the wings.

Until, of course, it wouldn't be like that. It would be awkwardly avoiding each other backstage. Making sure we never stopped at the same gas station. Standing silently at a Comfort Motel breakfast buffet as we both reached for the last mixed-berry yogurt.

Or maybe it wouldn't be like that. Maybe one of us would just leave, eventually, and I'd be the same as before, only with another little piece of my heart missing.

It wasn't worth the risk.

"I don't have time to get distracted," I said. "I need to focus on my music. And you, Boone Wyant, whatever else you are, would be an awfully big distraction."

"I guess I'll take that as a compliment?" He scratched his head. It was honestly unfair for someone to look this good. "Can we at least be friends?"

"Sure." I shrugged. "I mean, there's only so much bee talk I can handle with Pauly."

"Bee talk?" he repeated, incredulous.

"You'll learn."

"Come on. Let's go look at that statue over there." He

pointed down the beach, then held out his hand. I looked at it but didn't take it. "It's just a hand, Josie," he said. "Nothing romantic."

"Mmm, yeah, I love a good platonic hand hold. Classic move."

"Try it. You might like it."

I heaved a mighty sigh, but I took his hand, and we walked closer to the statue. It was a big, buff, green merman holding a trident, one hand on a sea turtle.

"Neptune," I read off a plaque bracketed by two bronze octopuses.

"That's basically what I look like without my shirt on," Boone joked.

"Honestly? I don't doubt it." He started to pull up the hem of his shirt. "That wasn't an invitation!" I tugged it right back down. "If you're expecting girlish shrieks of delight, please don't. I'm not one of your fangirls."

"They're called Baby Booners."

"Pardon?" I cupped my hand to my ear, sure I must have misheard him.

"My fans. They call themselves the Baby Booners." At least on repeating it he had the good sense to look embarrassed.

"You are kidding." I burst out laughing. "Stop, Boone, please tell me you're making this up." I placed a hand on the fence around the Neptune statue for balance. I was laughing so hard, I was worried I might fall over. "Baby Booners. I can't. That is absolutely unreal."

"It's not like I came up with it!" he protested. "They did!"

"Baby Booners. Oh man." I wheezed. "This is the best thing that's happened to me all day."

"*That* was the best thing to happen to you all day?" he pouted. "Ouch, Josie."

"Sorry, Romeo. Again: I'm not some swooning Baby Booner."

"Okay, that's it, you're going in." He walked toward me, a joking look of menace on his face.

"Going in what? The water?!" I gasped. "No way!"

I started sprinting down the beach, away from Boone, shrieking with laughter as he chased me. If he wanted to throw me in the ocean, he'd have to catch me first.

And I knew he could *never* catch me.

CHAPTER THIRTY-THREE
Katy

MY PHONE BUZZED NEXT TO me. Again. Hopefully it would just die soon. I didn't have time to talk to whoever was trying to reach me. Time was starting to run together. I had definitely fallen asleep at some point, but I wasn't quite sure what day it was anymore. It didn't matter. All that mattered was this dress.

Sighing, I held a black tassel up to the neckline, then held it back down again. What was I doing? I wasn't a tassel person! Or maybe I was? I didn't even know anymore. The more I added things, then took them away again, the more confused I got.

I had to get out of here. The walls were closing in on me, and the already small apartment was feeling so tiny it was suffocating me. Grabbing only my keys and my wallet, I fled down the stairs, out of the building, and ran for the subway, traveling uptown to the one place I always felt safe.

The Little Red Lighthouse was exactly what it sounded like—a small red lighthouse in Fort Washington Park, facing the Hudson River and nestled snugly beneath the George Washington Bridge. When I was little, Mom used to read me the picture book *The Little Red Lighthouse and the Great Gray Bridge*, and one day we'd traveled uptown to see it together. That became the first of many visits. We came when I needed to talk through a fight with a friend, or if I got upset about a bad grade, and later, when we needed to cry together about Mom's diagnosis. Even though the Little Red Lighthouse had its share of bad memories, too, it never failed to make me feel hopeful. Like as long as it could shine its light out over the Hudson, everything would be okay. It was my quiet place, my safe place, somewhere I could be alone with my thoughts.

Now it was where I came when I missed Mom most of all.

I could have visited the cemetery, I guess, but I felt closer to her here, on the water. Sighing, I sank down onto a bench and looked out over the river. What a mess I'd made of everything.

"Katy?"

I turned, and there he was. My knight in shining track pants. Watching KO jog toward me in his Western Queens Boxing Gym hoodie, I almost burst into tears right then and there.

The Little Red Lighthouse may have been my safe place, but KO was my safe person.

"KO?" I asked as he took a seat next to me. "What are you doing here?"

"What am I doing here? I'm looking for you!" He hugged me on the bench, crushing me to his chest, like he never wanted to let me go. "You missed our goodnight call. You didn't pick up. For the first time ever."

Oh no.

"I'm so sorry, KO." I couldn't believe I hadn't talked to him last night. "I didn't mean to make you worry."

"Of course I was worried! We've *never* gone to sleep without talking before. And I texted Jorge this morning, and he said you weren't responding to his texts, either, and then I really started to worry."

"I can't believe I didn't pick up. I was just so wrapped up in working on the dress for the Rex London fashion show, I forgot the rest of the world existed."

"That's what I thought might have happened. But nobody answered when I buzzed your apartment, so then I *really* got worried."

"We must have just missed each other. I haven't left my apartment since I went to Lacy's yesterday. How did you find me?"

"Because I know you, Katy." He smiled, his eyes crinkling, his face almost as familiar to me as my own. "I know this is your special place. Your safe place, that you always come to when you're worried. Because this is where you used to come with your mom."

Wordlessly, I reached over and grabbed his hand. We

sat on the bench like that, quietly, just being together, watching the water. It wasn't exactly a tropical beach—I certainly wasn't about to go swimming in there anytime soon—but it was my favorite view in the whole world.

"I miss her so much," I said.

"I know you do."

"I just feel like she'd know exactly what to do with the dress. She could tell me why it wasn't working and we'd figure it out together."

"What are you talking about?" KO frowned. "What's wrong with your dress?"

I realized then I hadn't told KO about how much I'd been struggling. Or Jorge, or anybody.

"My dress is a mess," I confessed. "And this isn't just me being too hard on myself or anything. Rex London said it was a disaster. Like, unless I pull off some kind of miracle, he's not even going to let me walk in the show. That kind of disaster."

"Oh man, Katy, I'm sorry." He pulled me close and squeezed. "I know you said that not all fashion risks pay off, and even the greats make mistakes, but that cannot have been easy to hear."

"It wasn't. But the worst part is, I agree with him! I know he's right. It *is* a mess. But I don't know how to fix it. It's just . . . for the first time ever, I can't figure out what I want to make. I can't figure out what I should design that's the most *me*. It's like I don't even know who I am anymore, or what that would look like on a dress form."

"That doesn't sound like you." KO frowned. "I don't know anything about fashion, but even I know that you have your very own Katy Keene sense of style. Like, I could look at anything you made and know instantly that *you* made it."

"That's how I used to feel, too. But right now, it feels like I forgot what that Katy Keene style is. That's why I wish that Mom was here." I had a small, creased picture of the two of us together that I'd been carrying around in my wallet like a totem. I pulled it out and smiled as I looked at it: Mom at the sewing machine, me in her lap. One of my earliest memories. "I need her to remind me who I am."

"You don't need her for that, Katy. You know who you are. Maybe . . ." He paused for a moment, thinking. "Maybe you just need her to remember what you love about fashion. Like, that little girl right there." He tapped the picture with his finger. "What's she thinking about?"

"Oh, man, I remember that day so well." I smiled. "That was the first time Mom trusted me to hold the fabric while she worked the pedal on the sewing machine with her feet. I felt so grown-up. I loved sewing with her so much." Tears pricked at my eyes, but these ones didn't hurt. "Taking pieces of fabric and turning them into clothing . . . it was like magic."

"Yeah. That's how you usually look when you talk about clothes," KO said happily. "Like they're magic."

"It was! It is. And she always had such a great sense of style, too." I looked at the clean, simple lines of Mom's dress, utterly elegant. "Although, I was pretty stylish, too," I joked, pointing at my overalls. "Look at all those little red heart appliqués."

"You were cute then and you're even cuter now."

"Look at all those little red heart appliqués," I said again, more slowly. I loved hearts. And red. Adding little bits of Katy-flair to other items of clothing I'd found or made or repurposed. Maybe I'd been shying away from doing my usual Katy thing because it didn't feel serious enough, or like something a designer would do. But I thought about Deja, and her awesome cat designs. She was doing incredible work while being exactly herself. It's not like cat faces were particularly serious. Why *couldn't* I create something that was more me?

My mind was whirling a million miles a minute, like it always did when I was really inspired. Maybe I would make a dress, but a new dress, something almost like what Mom was wearing with its elegant simplicity, but with a few fun Katy touches. Maybe cute pockets? Or fun buttons, like the strawberry ones I'd found at Lou Lou Buttons? And what would be the right hem length?

"Ladies and gentlemen, she's back!" KO announced like he was inside the ring at the boxing gym.

"Huh?" My mind was still on seams and pocket placement.

"I can see you thinking. I know how your mind works." He tapped the side of my head gently. "You know exactly what you're going to do."

"I do. I mean, I think I do." I grinned. "I need to sketch. Why didn't I bring my notebook?" I patted my coat pockets, pulling out a random pen. "Do you have anything to write on?"

KO pulled an insanely long receipt out of his pants pocket. Grinning, thinking of my mom at Lacy's all those years ago, I sketched like my hands were on fire, the dress in my mind taking shape on the paper before me.

"I love it." KO looked over my shoulder as I finished up the sketch.

"Yeah?" I examined it critically from every angle, but couldn't find fault with any of it. It was exactly what I wanted to make for Rex London's fashion show.

I'd be proud to walk any catwalk in this. Even at Lacy's.

Especially at Lacy's.

"I mean, you know I don't know anything about fashion, but I think it looks beautiful. And more than anything else, I love the way it made your face light up."

Carefully, I folded the receipt up and tucked it in my pocket. This might work. This might really work.

"Come on. Let's get out of here before it gets dark." KO hopped off the bench and held out his hands to pull me up. "Oh, wait a sec. Let me just tell Jorge I found you." He pulled out his phone and started texting. "Once I called Molly's Crisis and Darius confirmed you weren't there, I sent Jorge to Lacy's to look for you."

I had a sudden vision of a panicked Jorge popping in

and out of dressing rooms, calling my name, and cringed with guilt.

"I'm so sorry I caused everyone so much worry."

"Don't be sorry. We were worried because we love you. I'd comb every inch of this city looking for you, and I know Jorge would do the same."

I was so lucky to have them. I had lost Mom, and I knew that was a wound that would never fully heal, but I was still surrounded by so much love.

"Just answer your phone next time," he teased gently. "No matter how big the fashion emergency."

"I promise. From now on, I am always accessible. Well, mostly accessible," I amended. "I'm going back home to start sewing right now, and I have to focus, but I promise I'll call you before I go to bed."

If I went to bed. I had a feeling I might stay up all night. But I'd call KO either way. I definitely didn't want him and Jorge combing the streets of Manhattan, looking for me again.

"Right now? It sounds like you've been working literally nonstop for days. Why don't you take a break, Katy?"

"I can't take a break now!" I shook my head. "Are you kidding? The fashion show is only two days away! I need to get back to work, and fix things, and—"

"I think what you *really* need might be a break from all this designer drama. Just a little one. So why don't you come to the least fashionable place in New York? Come home with me."

"Oh, stop it." I laughed. "Your house is not the least fashionable place in New York."

True, Mrs. Kelly liked to cook in Crocs with socks, but who was I to judge? She could certainly cook circles around me. Maybe the Crocs were part of the culinary creative process.

"Think about how nice it might feel to relax, just for a couple hours. I've gotta stop by the boxing gym really quick, but after that, come have dinner with us. Mom's making pot roast. There'll be plenty."

"Ooh." I'd been living off a mostly-stale box of Triscuits for the past couple of days while I worked. A serving of Mrs. Kelly's famous pot roast with mashed potatoes sounded like exactly what I needed right now. As did being squished at the table among all the other Kellys, all teasing one another and cracking up and talking a mile a minute. And probably all wearing sweatpants. Maybe a break from couture wouldn't be the worst thing. "Now you're speaking my love language."

"I know. What did you say on our first Valentine's Day?"

"Don't get me flowers. Bring me some more of your mom's mashed potatoes."

"You love her more than me, don't you?" KO slung an arm around my shoulders as we walked away from the Little Red Lighthouse. I snuck one last glance at it as we left the park.

"It's not your fault. She's very lovable. And you've never made me a mashed potato."

"I'll mash you as many potatoes as you want, Katy Keene."

We talked about potatoes and the paperwork KO was grabbing before his next match and everything but my dress for Rex London's fashion show as we traveled to the Western Queens Boxing Gym.

Inside, the gym was missing its usual soundtrack of gloves smacking against bags and fighters grunting with effort. Instead, all we could hear was someone crying. Loudly. We followed the sound, until we found a small blonde figure curled up behind the ring, her head down and her knees tucked into her chest.

"Jinx?" KO asked. She didn't respond.

"Is she okay?" I hoped she hadn't been hurt somehow. We ran over to her quickly, her sobs getting louder.

"I'm so sorry I blew you off." KO knelt next to her, apologizing. "That was really lame of me. I was worried about Katy, but I should have at least texted you to let you know I wasn't coming."

"I'm not crying about you, you dummy!" Jinx lifted her head. Two black rivers of mascara-stained tears ran down her cheeks. "It's m-my girlfriend!"

"What did she do now?" KO looked like he'd like to use this girlfriend as a punching bag. He settled down, sitting next to Jinx. "Did she stand you up again?"

"No. And she'll never stand me up again. Because I saw her kissing someone else!" Jinx wailed.

"She cheated on you?" I gasped, sinking to the floor to

sit on Jinx's other side. Now I felt even sillier about how jealous I'd been of Jinx. Of course I'd had nothing to worry about. And here she was, with *her* heart broken, the poor thing. "Oh, Jinx, I'm so sorry."

"I guess she didn't technically cheat." Big, fat tears spilled out of Jinx's blue eyes. "We never said we were exclusive. I just assumed. Because we were spending so much time together over the last couple of weeks, and I was so crazy about her, I just assumed she was so crazy about m-m-m-me . . ." The rest of her sentence got lost in big, gulping sobs.

I put one arm around Jinx, and KO put his arm around her other side, and we wrapped her up in a hug. I'd had my heart broken by plenty of other things, but never by love. KO and I exchanged a glance over Jinx's head. I was so lucky to have him. I knew he would never break my heart like this, not ever. Forget the Little Red Lighthouse. KO was my safe place. I could count on him, always, no matter what.

"Let me get you some tissues," I offered as KO talked to Jinx in a soothing voice. I popped up and hunted around until I found a box of tissues at the front desk.

"She didn't even care enough to tell me herself that it was over." Jinx reached out to take a tissue from the box I held. "Can you believe that? I had to read about it on some *blog*. And they had pictures, too, so I knew it wasn't made up."

A blog? I shot KO a quizzical look.

"Jinx's girlfriend—ex-girlfriend—is kind of famous, I guess," KO said in an undertone as Jinx continued to blow her nose. "But I don't know who she is. Jinx wouldn't even tell me her name or show me a picture."

"Well." I cleared my throat. "Sounds like good riddance to bad rubbish, anyway. You're beautiful and kind and lethal, and you're gonna be so much better off without her, Jinx."

"Then why does it hurt so much?" she asked in a small voice.

"Because loss always hurts." I hugged her. "But it'll get better with time. Everything does. And you know what else might help?"

"What?" Jinx hiccupped.

"Mashed potatoes." KO and I locked eyes and smiled. "Do you think your mom has room for one more at the table?"

"You know she always does. Come on, Jinx." KO helped her up, and I scrambled to my feet beside them. "Let's go eat like there's no weigh-in tomorrow."

Right now, it was time for dinner.

Tonight, it would be time to sew.

And I couldn't wait to get started.

CHAPTER THIRTY-FOUR
Jorge

"WELL, WELL, WELL. LOOK WHO finally decided to show her face." Darius paused in wiping down the bar as I walked into Molly's Crisis. "Pardon me saying so, but girl, you look awful."

I looked down at my Trenton Thunder sweatpants—a gift from Hugo after he'd been signed to the Trenton Thunder, the Yankees' AA farm team—and my *West Side Story* sweatshirt from high school, with holes for the thumbs and a fine misting of Cheetos dust around the tummy area.

Awful was probably an understatement. I went to run a hand through my hair and pulled out a Cheeto.

"Well." I took a seat at the bar, looking at Darius's unmade face. "You're not exactly beat yourself at the moment."

"How dare you. I'm letting my skin *breathe*. Living life as the fabulous Miss Pixie Velvet does take a toll on the pores, honey." He pushed his rag off to the side. "Even the most noncomedogenic foundation clogs eventually. Now. Where have you been hiding, why have you been hiding, and for the love of all that is holy, where is it you've been that has so many Cheetos?"

"My family's bodega." There was something itching the back of my neck. I reached into the collar of my sweatshirt and pulled out another Cheeto. I contemplated eating it, but that was a line I wasn't ready to cross. "I mean, mostly I was in my room. But we've got a lot of Cheetos downstairs. Ma kept yelling at me about eating all our profits, but, whatever."

"And why were you hiding in your room, Broadway baby?" he prompted.

"That's why."

"I see." Darius pulled out a glass, filled it to the brim with ginger ale, and slid it across the bar to me. I drank deeply. "Also, who are you with all these ginger ales? Some little old man?"

"I like ginger ale, okay! It's not a crime!"

"It's a weird signature drink."

"Are you offering me something stronger?"

"Try me again in three years, baby. So, let me see if I got this right: You didn't get cast in *Hello, Dolly!*, you've been hiding up in Washington Heights, and now you're sitting here in front of me in a truly tragic ensemble, drinking little old man juice and covered in the world's orangest snack food."

"That pretty much sums it up. Except you didn't make me sound pathetic enough."

"Jorge. You are not pathetic," Darius said, suddenly serious. "You're an actor. Actors get rejected. It's part of the process. Does it hurt? Oh yeah. It's the *worst*. But that doesn't make you pathetic, or mean you stop trying. I've seen you dance. And even when you're just singing, casually, here at the bar with Katy, I can hear that you've got something. You've got *it*. And if you want to make this happen, you can. It just might take a little more time than you'd like."

"They said I was too soft." I watched the bubbles in my ginger ale float up to the surface. "Not masculine enough. Too . . . gay."

"Well, screw them and the surrey with the fringe on top they rode in on," Darius snapped, angry. "You're not too any of those things. There's no such thing as being too soft or too gay. And if they think that's a problem, that's *their* problem, not yours. And let me tell you something else. I saw that Ethan Fox meat show. Nothing but stank and overacting. That man could not be more overrated." Darius snorted. "At least here, when we overact, we do it on purpose."

"Thanks." Darius was a performer, too. And he probably knew all about being told he was too something. It was nice not to feel like I was alone.

"You're welcome. Now, let me fix your face."

"What's wrong with it?" I touched my cheek self-consciously, rubbing at what was almost definitely orange dust.

"What isn't." Darius shot me a look. "I don't have the right shade to do your foundation, but how about a little eye makeup?"

"Sure." I shrugged. The Cheetos definitely hadn't made me feel better. Maybe a new face would.

Darius went backstage and returned with his makeup box. It was an old-school Caboodle with a clear purple top, like the kind Ma used to keep her makeup in back when she was on the pageant circuit as Miss Puerto Rico. He hopped up onto the barstool next to me, brandishing a brush.

I'd played around with makeup before—Ma's when I was little, Katy's when I was older. I could even execute a pretty decent smoky eye, thanks to YouTube tutorials. But I'd never sat and had someone else do it for me. Sitting in the quiet bar, Barbra warbling on low in the background, with Darius's makeup brush swishing across my face, was actually kind of meditative. I cleared my mind, let go of Ethan Fox and everything *Hello, Dolly!*, and just sat there.

I hadn't expected that makeup would be the thing that helped me finally turn my brain off, but I'd take whatever worked.

"Done." I opened my eyes to see Darius rustling around in his Caboodle. "Got it." Triumphantly, he pulled out a small plastic hand mirror edged in lavender glitter. I think Ma had that one, too. "So?" He held it up expectantly. "What do you think?"

What did I think? *What did I think?* I didn't even know what to think! Compared with this, the playing around with makeup I'd done had literally been playing around. Like a total clown. This was different. This was *art*.

With one finger, I traced the high, arched line of my penciled-in brows. My eyes looked enormous, framed by a swishy flick of thick black liner and Bambi-like fake eyelashes. Maybe the best part of all was the bright red lip. Total old-school Hollywood vibes. It made me think of Katy's coat, the one with the Peter Pan collar. But it made me *feel* powerful.

But the thing I loved best of all? I still looked like *me*.

"Can you teach me how to do this?" I demanded.

"Can I? Yes. Will I?" Darius cocked his head, deliberating. "I'll think about it."

He would, though. I knew he would. I could tell from the way he was trying not to smile as he bustled back behind the bar, Caboodle in hand.

The door blew open, letting in a gust of wind and one Miss Katy Keene, wearing plaid pajama pants, a Western Queens Boxing Gym sweatshirt, and an enormous grin.

"Well, well, well. I haven't seen this one in forever, either!" Darius exclaimed as he returned. "And here I thought I'd gotten lucky and you two had decided to stop bothering me."

"Wow. Jorge. You look stunning." Katy stopped in her tracks. "Like, literally stunning."

"Thank you." Darius preened. "I'm very good."

"This outfit is . . . something," she said diplomatically as she crossed toward me, "but your *face*."

"Are we talking about *my* outfit?" She was covered in what I liked to think of as fashion debris, little threads and scraps and who knows what else. I started plucking little bits of fabric out of her hair like a monkey. "You're wearing pajamas."

"I am?" She looked down at her legs, stunned, like she had no idea she'd left the house in them. "Huh. Well. Doesn't matter! I need to show you my dress! It's good. I think. Really good. But I need you to look at it and tell me it's good. Except . . . wait a minute." Brow furrowing suspiciously, she reached up and pulled a Cheeto out of the collar of my sweatshirt. Another one? Seriously?! How many were hiding on me?! "Oh, Jorge." Her face crumpled. "You didn't get the part."

Of course she'd known. I remembered sitting on Katy's living room floor freshman year, crying and elbow-deep in a bag of Cheetos, because they'd given the role of Cinderella's Prince in *Into the Woods* to some no-talent senior with a weak chin. Ugh.

"That part didn't deserve him," Darius said as Katy wrapped her arms around my middle. "Look at that face. He's going to be a star. And he doesn't need Ethan Fox to do it."

"Darius is right. I *am* gonna be a star," I vowed. I probably still had a couple days of Cheetos left—grief is a process, y'all—but I wouldn't let this one setback stop me. I couldn't. I'd had the same dream since I was four years old when Ma took me to see *Peter Pan*, and I realized that was what I wanted to do: fly. And that's exactly how I felt when I was onstage. Like I was flying. I wasn't going to stop chasing that feeling because of some pretentious director with outdated ideas about conventional masculinity who thought high art meant serving people *stew*.

Katy hugged me tighter, and I squeezed her back.

"Now," I cleared my throat, "did you say something about a dress?"

CHAPTER THIRTY-FIVE
Pepper

"BYE, BYE, BLONDIE!"

by Amelie Stafford for *CelebutanteTalk*,
a subsidiary of Cabot Media

Guess blondes don't have more fun—or maybe they aren't fun *enough* for the perfectly passionate Pepper Smith!

After being spotted out on the town several times with the same, still-unidentified mystery blonde, it appears that Pep has sent her packing. Last night, Pepper was spotted locking lips outside ultra-exclusive nightclub La Piscine with celebrity YouTuber Auden Grace. Auden's channel, where he livestreams himself playing video games, has nearly one hundred million subscribers—and if he keeps seeing the sensational Miss Smith, who knows what records he might break! Perhaps his channel might soon feature a cameo from the popular Pep herself! We're sure she'd get the high score in anything she attempted!

Well, mystery blonde, wherever you are tonight, know that the rest of New York is crying into their pillows right along with you—well, everyone except for lucky, lucky Auden Grace!

CHAPTER THIRTY-SIX
Josie

BOONE WYANT WASN'T GREAT AT BEING FRIENDS.

Don't get me wrong, he was plenty friendly. Problem was, he was *more* than friendly.

"Dang, Josie." He whistled at me as we stood backstage at the Buccaneer in Greenville, North Carolina, giving my black crop top a very appreciative glance. "Are you trying to kill me?"

Wasn't trying to kill him. Although if he kept this up, I might have to. When I told him I just wanted to be friends back in Virginia Beach, I wasn't playing hard to get. I wanted to focus on my music, and just my music. Full stop. But Boone was being even *more* distracting now than he'd been when we were just flirting at Biscuit Barrels.

In Fayetteville, he—surprise!—invited me onstage to sing with him. The song turned out to be Bonnie Raitt's

"I Can't Make You Love Me." Cue massive eye roll. After singing to a crowd of Baby Booners who looked like they wanted to murder me, and a slew of middle-aged jazz fans who looked surprised to be enjoying themselves so much, I made it clear that he was *never* to do that again.

So he just started dedicating the song to me instead.

I was starting to get the sense that Boone hadn't been told "no" a lot in his life. He was charming, sure, but now that his charm offensive wasn't working on me, it appeared to have short-circuited his brain. That boy was doing too much, and I was over it.

"You can't make your heart feel something it won't," Pauly warbled as we walked down the hall of the Comfort Motel Charlotte, in search of the vending machine and some ice.

"Pauly, I swear." I held up my hand for silence. "That is the *last* song I want to hear right now."

It's hard to look scary in a leopard-print onesie, but it must have worked, because Pauly scurried away without another word from Bonnie Raitt, abandoning the vending machine.

This leopard print zip-up onesie was the most ridiculous garment I owned, but it was so comfortable, I didn't care. Melody had bought them for me and Val for Christmas one year as a joke, and when I'd been packing up to leave Riverdale, I couldn't quite bear to leave it behind, even though the Pussycats had been long gone by that point. It brought back too many good memories of sharing popcorn in Val's basement, critiquing all the singers on different reality TV shows, and imagining all the ways we were gonna take the world by storm.

Roaming the halls of a Comfort Motel in a leopard print onesie and fuzzy slippers wasn't exactly what I'd imagined in those days, but if I'd learned anything since being on the road with Dad, it was that working, really working as a professional musician, wasn't all nonstop glamour. Of course, there had been some incredible days and awesome shows, but if I saw one more Comfort Motel orange lobby throw pillow, I was going to lose my mind.

Sighing, I switched the ice bucket to my other side. I'd stepped weird while walking off stage tonight—so unlike me; I practically lived in heels—and now my ankle was killing me. Lucky for me, this appeared to be the one Comfort Motel in all of creation that didn't have the exact same layout as all the others, and I was having the worst time finding the stupid ice machine.

Limping around the corner, I almost walked straight into a couple kissing. Oh my god. Seriously, people? This was a *motel*. You could literally get a room. Any room. No excuse for PDA.

I was about to go and search for the ice machine down a less-occupied hall, but then realized that although I didn't recognize the woman in the tiny shorts with the long blonde hair, I definitely recognized the guy.

He was still wearing the cowboy hat he'd performed in that night.

"Wow." I settled my ice bucket on my hip. "Are you serious right now?"

Boone stopped kissing whoever it was and turned to look at me. There was an expression on his face I couldn't quite read.

"Wait for me inside, darlin'?" Boone tipped his hat back on his forehead and handed the giggling blonde his room key. She kissed it—unbelievable—then disappeared into the room. "Do we have a problem here, Josie? Because for the life of me, I can't think of what that problem would be."

"Did you pick up a *groupie*?" I hissed. "Really classy, Boone. Wow."

"So what if I did?" His tone was defensive, and his stance was trying a little too hard to be casual. "I don't see why you care. You made it very clear that nothing was going to happen between us."

"So you *immediately* jump on the next warm body you find?"

"I didn't jump on anything! But if I did, I don't see how that's any of your business! I gave you plenty of chances to change your mind, and all you told me was *stop*. So this is me. Stopping."

We glared at each other. I didn't know why this was bothering me so much. I *didn't* want to start anything with Boone Wyant, and this incident was exactly *why* I didn't want to. I couldn't open myself up to getting hurt by someone I was working with. Especially someone who was in a different city every night, surrounded by women who were literally obsessed with him. It would be way too messy.

We were barely even friends. Really, we were just colleagues. Coworkers could make out with blonde women if they wanted to. Plus, he'd been pissing me off all over North Carolina, with those stupid romantic gestures, which weren't romantic since I *didn't want them*! So why did I care? I'd told him to stop pursuing me, and clearly, he had. Maybe it was just how fast he'd moved on. It was kind of a blow to the ego.

Or maybe, a little voice inside said, *he made you feel special*.

Ugh. Forget that. I was Josie McCoy. I *was* special. And not because of some Instagram cowboy with a guitar. I was special because of my voice and my drive and my heart, and Boone Wyant didn't deserve any of that.

"You know what?" I said slowly. "You're right. It isn't any of my business."

"Josie—"

"Knock yourself out, Boone." I turned to go, in search of ice machines and then back to my room, where I could hopefully forget about all this and sleep.

"Come on, Josie, don't be like that," he called after me.

"Be like what? I'm not being like anything!" I was still talking to him, but I wouldn't face him. I continued my undignified trek down the hall, onesie, fuzzy slippers, ice bucket, and all. "Night, Boone." I waved sarcastically behind me.

Safely around the corner, I paused for a moment.

He didn't come after me.

Not that I wanted him to.

But he didn't.

CHAPTER THIRTY-SEVEN
Katy

THE PERFUME HALL AT LACY'S had been transformed. Everything that wasn't nailed down had been pushed to the side, creating an aisle lined with two rows of black folding chairs on either side. There was a temporary lighting rig set up around the chandelier, casting dramatic shadows over the space. And in the back, in front of the grand staircase up a half level to the shoe department, floor-to-ceiling curtains, printed with a "Rex London x Lacy's" logo, hung to create a backstage area for the models—er, designers—to emerge from. Instead of the normal bustle of perfume spritzers, the hallway was deserted, everything set up and ready to go. I hurried down the catwalk to the elevators, hoping I'd be back to walk the runway as part of my show, instead of slinking down it in defeat.

No. The dress was *good*. I knew it was. And if Rex London didn't like it for whatever reason, I'd wear it out to Franca's, where KO and I would split the two slices and can of Coke $1.99 special.

Either way, I would be fine.

I *was* fine.

But that didn't stop my heart from beating a nervous, rapid rhythm as the elevator climbed up to the sixth floor.

Here was the chaos I'd been expecting downstairs. All the designers were running around in various stages of dress, some applying makeup in front of the three-way mirror. In the middle of the room, Rex London was gesticulating with a pair of scissors—always a dangerous proposition—a pincushion on his wrist. At his side, Andy was frantically checking things off on a clipboard.

"Howard, if I see one more thread sticking out of the hem of your pants, so help me . . ." Rex threatened. "There is no room for sloppiness in couture!"

In the middle of berating Howard, Rex and Andy turned toward the door and saw me. They both stopped what they were doing and stared. Actually, it felt like the formerly chaotic room had all come to a quiet standstill. I hovered anxiously in the doorway, unsure if I should come in or not.

"Well. If it isn't Katy Keene." Did he like it? I couldn't read anything in his face or the tone of his voice. "So this is it? This is the dress?"

"This is the dress." I'd worn it over, risking who knew what kind of staining on the subway, but having it on had given me an extra boost of confidence. As did my favorite pair of T-strap shoes with the rounded red toe and the nude heels. Getting all the city grime off the shoes had been almost as much work as making the dress itself.

"Come in, come in." He waved me into the room. "Up in front of the mirror, please."

Rex and Andy circled me like two sharks as I stood on the dais. It took every ounce of self-control I possessed not to wipe my sweaty hands on the dress and stain the silk.

"Well, that color certainly isn't shy," Rex said eventually.

Maybe red had been a mistake. But I always felt most myself in red. And if I was going to mess this up, I was going to mess this up as *me*. That was the mistake I'd made right from the start: forgetting who I was. Or being afraid to show the world exactly who I was. Whether I was walking in a fashion show or eating a slice at Franca's, from now on, I was going to wear what made me happy, and not worry so much about making things perfect. That was the whole point of fashion, after all: self-expression.

"The silhouette is almost '40s inspired, with those little structured sleeves, but you've kept it more modern by making the lines softer. Usually I hate a sweetheart neckline, but it's working here. The draping on the skirt is impeccable. And the pockets as hearts . . ." He smiled, and my heart lifted with hope. "It's an inspired touch."

"It's a little cutesy, don't you think?" Andy whispered behind his hand.

"It's a lot cutesy. But have you looked at this person? She's cutesy personified." I was trying to decide whether or not I was offended. "Would I sell this dress? No. It's not a Rex London design. But that doesn't matter. This dress tells me who *you* are, Katy Keene. And I love it. And I think there are a lot of women out there who would love it, too."

I glowed with happiness and pride. Finally, I'd found myself again.

"So . . . I can walk?" I asked tentatively.

"Yes, you can walk. And keep in touch, okay?" Rex said. "If you keep churning out looks like this, you should have the start of a nice cohesive collection. Let me know when you can show me more, and maybe I'll be able to help."

"Really?" I squeaked. "That is so nice of you. Thank you."

"That's why I'm doing this show, Katy. I don't need the publicity. Trust me, Rex London is doing more than well enough."

"We're on track to outperform Marc Jacobs this year," Andy said smugly.

"Shh, Andy, let's not malign the old guard." Winking, Rex held a finger to his lips. "But I remember what it was like to be starting out. Unsure of how to make my dreams a reality. Unsure of who I was, what to do, or how to begin. School helped a lot, but I could have used a mentor. Are you enrolled anywhere right now?"

"Not right now. I've always dreamed of going to Parsons, but it just didn't happen this year . . ."

"Well, think about school. In the meantime, get a job in the industry. You have a lot to learn, Katy Keene," he said seriously. I nodded. I knew I did. "But I think you could do great things."

That settled it. I was getting a job here, at Lacy's, and it would be the first step toward making everything happen for me. I could do this. I knew I could.

"Now. Howard!" he announced. "Show me your hems!"

A miserable-looking guy sitting in a chair stuck out his pant legs as Rex hurried over to him.

"Rex is really unusual, you know," Andy said, once it was just the two of us alone in the middle of the room. "It's one of the reasons I wanted to work with him so badly."

"I know. His tailoring is unreal, especially in his ready-to-wear line. What he's done for workwear—"

"I'm not talking about his designs." Andy shook his head. "He's an unusual person in this industry because he really, truly cares about helping the next generation. And he's kind. But most unusually of all," he continued, "Rex gives second chances. If this show had been run by anyone else, you *never* would have been allowed back. Not even on a trial basis. And it probably would have ended your career before it even began."

"I know." I hung my head. "I know how lucky I am. I'm not taking any of this for granted."

"You got a second chance, Katy Keene." He smiled. "Make the most of it."

"I will," I promised. I couldn't do this *with* Mom. But I could do it *for* her. And I was going to make the most of every single chance I got.

In seemingly no time at all, we were standing backstage. The crowd outside sounded unbelievably loud. It must have been packed. Was I really about to walk out there in front of all these people?

The beginning of the show passed in a blur of nerves. Rex went out to speak to the audience, Andy lined us up, and the first designers began to walk. This was it. It was really happening!

"And that's you, Katy Keene," Andy said, holding the mouthpiece of his headset. "Go. Go. Go!"

I emerged from behind the curtains, almost blinded by lights after the dark of backstage. For a second, I paused, trying to get my bearings, and then, I saw them in the distance. The famous Lacy's stained-glass windows, designed by Louis Comfort Tiffany himself. Smiling, I picked out a small red stained-glass flower, focused on it, just like Jorge had taught me, and began to walk.

And even though I'd been dreading it, it actually turned out to be kind of . . . fun? No, scratch that, it was *really* fun. I'd been watching fashion shows for so long, and now I was actually part of one! Don't get me wrong, I had no desire to become a professional model—plus I was about a foot too short—but stomping down the runway, in a dress I was proud to wear, was truly a once-in-a-lifetime experience. This was something above and beyond the wildest dreams of little girl Katy. She would have loved this so much.

And I knew Mom would have loved it, too.

Halfway down the catwalk, I felt confident enough to sneak a peek at the audience. There, in the front row, was KO. Surrounded by all the fashionistas in their daring looks, he looked slightly out of place in the suit he'd worn to graduation, but I loved him for making the effort to dress up. Our eyes locked, he smiled, and he mouthed "gorgeous" at me.

Jinx sat on one side of KO, fitting right in with the other black-clad fashion people in her black jeans and leather jacket, and on KO's other side, Jorge was resplendent in a velvet smoking jacket worn over a bare chest with a loosely tied cravat, his curly hair wild. Jorge pretended to collapse into his chair, mouthing, "You've slain me!"

I'd been so wrapped up with meeting with Rex that I hadn't even texted my friends to confirm that I'd be walking in the show, but they'd been here anyway, early enough to get front-row seats, confident that my dress would be good enough. That's how much they believed in me. How could one girl be so lucky?

I reached the end of the runway and posed, hitting three looks. Maybe Jorge should add in a side hustle as a professional modeling coach, because I had to admit, I felt pretty fabulous. Now all I had to do was make it backstage with-out tripping.

Exchanging grins with Deja as she headed out next, I made it safely backstage. I hadn't embarrassed myself at all! In fact, I thought I'd actually done myself proud. And I'd done Mom proud, too.

Oh, right. And there was one final walk. I'd barely made it backstage before Andy started hustling me back into line behind the designers who'd gone before me. Once Deja made it backstage, Andy slotted her into place behind me. Rex London led us out, a parade of all the designers, basking in the applause. Even before I saw my friends again, I could hear Jorge cheering louder than everyone else. He'd always been able to project phenome-nally well.

After brief congratulations from Rex, he released us into the crowd. Bobbing and weaving my way through people chatting excitedly, I ran straight into KO's arms.

"Katy!" He lifted me up off the floor. "Your dress is beautiful. *You* are beautiful." Setting me down, he kissed the top of my head. "I'm so proud of you."

"Katy-girl, you *slayed* out there." Jorge hugged me from my other side. "I am literally deceased. That was epic. I should probably become a runway coach."

"That's what I was thinking!" I squealed.

"Also, do you know if the cutie in the suit is single?"

"Howard?" Maybe his night was about to turn around. "Not sure. But you should *definitely* go ask."

After briefly fluffing up his hair, Jorge left in pursuit of Howard. I scanned the crowd, but I didn't see Veronica's sleek dark hair anywhere. Sure enough, when I checked my phone, there was a text from V, apologizing for missing the show due to an "entrepreneurial emergency."

Whatever it was, I knew it must have been important. And of course I wasn't upset that she missed the show! Veronica had given me such a gift already by recommending me to Rex—there was nothing more I could ask of her.

"I got you flowers." KO bent down to pull a slightly squashed bouquet of roses out from under his chair. "Maybe I wasn't supposed to? I didn't see anybody else with flowers, but we'd always bring them for my sisters' piano recitals, so I thought—"

"I love them." Pulling them to my nose, I inhaled deeply. "That was so sweet. Thank you." He really was the absolute best. "How's Jinx doing?" I'd seen her during the show but couldn't find her now. "Is she holding up okay?"

"I think so." KO turned me by my shoulders so I was facing behind me.

"Well. She seems like she's doing better," I murmured, watching Jinx talk animatedly with Deja.

"Oh yeah, she's better than better," KO said, his tone wistful. "She got a call today inviting her to go train at Joe Frazier's gym."

"Smokin' Joe?" I didn't know a lot about boxing, but I did know the name of one of KO's all-time favorite boxers. "His gym's in Philadelphia, right?"

"Yeah. Jinx is leaving as soon as she gets her stuff packed up. Like, within the next couple days. And I'm so happy for her; it's an amazing opportunity, but . . ."

"But you're a little jealous, too," I filled in the blanks for him. He flushed, like he was ashamed to admit it. "That's totally understandable. Don't feel bad. You're human, KO."

"I know. I just don't want Jinx to think I'm anything less than thrilled about it. She's an incredible fighter and she deserves this, but it's hard to see her go. Not just because I'll miss her, but because I've always wanted to train there, too."

"And you will. Someday. I know it." I squeezed his hand. "Then you'll be fighting at Madison Square Garden."

"And you'll be selling your designs on Madison Avenue."

"And this'll be our city." I turned to him, winding my arms around his neck.

"It already is, Katy." He leaned down, his mouth mere moments away from mine. "It's always been our kind of town."

We kissed, and I felt my insides fizzing like soda bubbles. I had the best guy, the best friends, and this dress was the first step in all of my designer dreams coming true.

"Excuse me, are you allowed to kiss in Lacy's?" Jorge interrupted us. I turned to see him facing us with his hands on his hips. Jinx stood behind him, smirking. "I thought this was a classy establishment."

"How about we go somewhere a little less classy?" I suggested.

"Someplace where the floors are always sticky?" Jorge said hopefully.

"And the soda's always flat?" I smiled.

"Wow, I don't know what you guys are talking about, but I'm sold," Jinx said sarcastically.

"Trust me, honey, you're gonna love it." Jorge threaded his arm through hers.

"Does Howard want to come?" I teased.

"Boyfriend up in Ithaca for grad school." Jorge pouted. "On to the next one."

"Are you sure you don't want to stick around a little longer?" KO asked. "Maybe see if there's someone you could ask about a job? I know working here has always been a dream."

"Don't worry. I'm coming back tomorrow, and I'm not leaving until I'm Lacy's newest employee," I said with determination.

"Then maybe after that, we'll hit up the apple orchard?" KO suggested. "I promised my girl some fall fun, and I always keep my promises."

"You always do." One of the many reasons I loved him. "Apples tomorrow. But tonight, there's only one place I want to celebrate."

CHAPTER THIRTY-EIGHT
Jorge

KATY, KO, JINX, AND I spilled into Molly's Crisis, four more people joining the dancing, sweaty crowd. The bar was absolutely packed, wall to wall with people of every color and size and expression of gender identity. Surrounded by all this glitter and gorgeousness, all these people being exactly who they were, I was home.

"I'm obsessed!" Jinx shouted over the chatter of the crowd and blare of early '00s Britney coming from the stage. "Why haven't I been here before? Why did I only find out about this place right before I'm leaving?! KO, you've been holding out on me!"

A new group of people entered the bar, pushing us farther into the room. Along the back wall, one of the high tops was miraculously open. There was a small piece of paper folded on top. I picked it up and read: "RESERVED for fashion icon Katy Keene and future Broadway star

Jorge Lopez (screw Ethan Fox xoxo) and Friends."

"They didn't," Katy read the sign over my shoulder. "Do you think that was Darius? He's too cute."

"Don't let him hear you say that," I warned her. "He's got a grumpy reputation to protect."

"First round's on me!" KO offered as Katy and I clambered up onto the seats. Jinx had already disappeared into the crowd, but I thought I saw her short blonde head bopping up and down as she danced with abandon. KO took our drink orders and shouldered his way through the crowd to the bar.

"Hi." Katy leaned forward so I could hear her above the noise, propping her elbows up on the high top. "How are you doing?"

"Na-unh. Nope. No way. I am shutting all this down right now." I waved a finger in her face. "Tonight is about celebrating you and your triumph and that gorgeous dress. Not about me being tragic."

"You are not tragic!" Katy exclaimed. "Stop being so hard on yourself. It was *one* audition. And it sounds like it wasn't really right for you, anyway."

"It probably wasn't," I agreed, "but the idea of skipping all those steps was so appealing. Just, like, one open call and boom, Equity. Broadway. Everything I've ever wanted, all my dreams coming true, just like that. Like magic."

"Maybe all those steps is what makes it magic," Katy said thoughtfully. "All the trying and the failing. Like, I know things ended up working out okay with the fashion show today—"

"Better than okay," I interrupted her. "Don't sell yourself short. You slayed that runway."

"Why, thank you." She bowed at the table. "But before that, I bombed. Big-time. You should have seen what I initially showed Rex . . . it was totally humiliating. And I think what I realized is that I'll probably have a lot more humiliating moments going forward in my career. But that's okay, because I'll learn from them. And what I learned this time is that I do my best work when I remember who I am. What makes me special. When I pay attention to what *I* have to say. And I think that's true about you, too." She leaned even closer. "You're a great performer always, no matter what. But you're a *star* when you're yourself."

I didn't just love Katy like family. She *was* family.

"I love you, Katy-girl."

"I know." She wrapped me up in a hug. "I love you, too."

In the middle of our hugfest, KO returned from the bar. He dropped off my ginger ale and placed something truly horrifying in front of Katy.

"Katy. Girl. What is happening here?" I disentangled myself from the hug, aghast at what was on the high top. "Did you just get a glass of maraschino cherries?"

"I know what my girl likes!" KO slung his arm around her. They were such a hetero throwback, but man they were cute. "There's a little bit of Coke down there, too."

"My signature drink." Katy tilted up her head to kiss him on the cheek. "Maraschino cherries, splash of Coke."

"Somehow I don't think that one's gonna catch on." I raised an eyebrow.

"Says the Ginger Ale King," she teased. "Maybe mine will catch on, when you're a bartender here." She smiled. "You can call it the 'Katy-girl.'"

"I don't know if I'll ever work here," I said doubtfully. "I'll probably be stuck at the bodega, restocking shelves and working the register and burning sandwiches on the flat top for the rest of my days. Darius doesn't seem that into it."

"I have a feeling he'll change his tune," she said confidently. "I don't know, I just . . . I can just see you working here. It feels right. And I'm not just saying that because I'd like a hookup for free maraschino cherries."

"There's Jinx," KO said. "Let me go see if she wants anything. She's gotta stay hydrated if she's gonna impress the team at Joe Frazier's."

"Who? Where?" I asked as KO left.

"Boxing stuff. Jinx is moving to Philly. Don't worry about it." Katy waved her hand. "Back to you."

"Hello? What did I just say? Tonight is about *you*."

"I got enough applause earlier. I want to know what you're going to do next."

"Keep auditioning." I was surprised by how quickly I said it, but happy to realize that rejection hadn't crushed me completely. "Broadway is where I belong. I'm gonna renew my *Backstage* subscription, and keeping taking classes at

Broadway Dance Center, and I'll audition for anything and everything. It might take a little longer to get to Broadway, but I'll get there. Someday. I know I will."

"Good." She grinned. "I'm really happy to hear that."

"You know what?" I said slowly, finally understanding something. "I think I realized what the problem is."

"What's that?" Katy asked.

"It's *revivals*."

"Explain," she prompted me.

"I still love musical theatre and performing, and I want to be on Broadway, but I want to originate a role in a *new* musical. Or if I do a revival, I want to be part of building the show from the ground up so I can create a role that is totally my own. A *show* that is totally my own. I'm tired of the people behind the table having all the power. I have something to say, too."

"I love that." Katy grabbed my hand and squeezed. "You're going to be a star, Jorge, I know it. And you deserve to do that on your own terms."

We clapped as the Britney-medley act finished, and then Darius came out onto the stage, in full drag as Pixie Velvet. Her face was beat for the gods, with glimmering bronze eye shadow and lashes out to there. And that itty-bitty waist was snatched in a blue-velvet rhinestone bodysuit.

"Is that the jumpsuit you were working on?" I asked Katy.

"Yes!" she squealed excitedly. "It looks so good! I love the way the rhinestones catch the stage lights."

"Maybe this is how you make rent money. Start charging these queens for repairing their costumes!"

"I couldn't." Katy shook her head. "They've given me so much by letting me hang out here in Molly's Crisis. And besides, I love it. It feels wrong to charge them."

We turned back to the stage. The grumpy bartender we knew and loved was gone, replaced by a queen in every sense of the word. She looked gorgeous, but more than that, she looked so *free*. Like she knew exactly who she was.

I wondered what that would feel like.

Why did I have to wonder? As the music started to play, and Pixie Velvet shook her hips in time to the beat, I sat very still in my chair, struck by a sudden realization. I could do this. I could do drag. What was stopping me from trying? Lord knew I was more than pretty enough. And had enough stage presence to fill this whole bar. I should be up there, too. But not as Jorge. As a different side of me, one I hadn't quite discovered yet.

But I couldn't wait to find her.

From the stage, Pixie Velvet belted out "I Wanna Dance With Somebody."

The music moved through me, in me, calling to me. Whitney was a queen for a reason.

"Come on, Jorge!" Katy pulled me to my feet. "Put down the ginger ale and let's dance!"

Ginger. I liked the sound of that.

And so we danced.

CHAPTER THIRTY-NINE
Pepper

FizzFeed

PEPPER SMITH CLAPS BACK AT FASHION WEEK BS

Absolute Icon Pepper Smith keeps it real on Instagram

Tatiana Trang

FizzFeed Staff

Legend Pepper Smith came for Fashion Week on Instagram, and as always, she held nothing back. Last night, Pepper posted a gorge B&W photo (so classic!) of herself posing on the High Line with an absolutely savage caption. Pep wrote that "I've decided Fashion Week is over. Haven't seen a single show this year and don't plan to see any." But before you freak out about NYFW getting canceled—check out what she wrote next: "Fashion shouldn't just be a week, inaccessible to all but the privileged few." That's the Pepper we know and love! And I think we can all agree that she. Is. Right.

Pepper signed off with a sweet note to her followers, saying, "This city is your runway. Walk it." And walk it she did. Pepper came ready to slay in a color-blocked swing coat with faux fur collar, a bold lip, and, of course, her signature specs (we love a girl who rocks glasses!). This look has us literally dead. The only thing brighter than the city lights is Pepper herself!

Check out her post on Instagram yourself—and get ready to walk your runway!

Instagram was an absolute load of rot. Sighing, I rolled over in bed, narrowly avoiding squishing the Jacques Torres chocolates I'd been consuming for the better part of an hour. Could I have been any more of a cliché? The king-size bed at the Five Seasons may have been dressed with the finest of luxury linens and the truffles were divine gourmet confections, but at the end of the day, I was still just a girl, lying in bed with chocolate, refusing to get out of her pajamas after a breakup.

Ending things with Jules had absolutely been the right call—as soon as she mentioned her mother, I knew we were over—but it had knocked me for more of a loop than I'd expected. Especially after I saw on Instagram that she was moving to Philly, so even if I *wanted* to make things work, it was no longer an option. I found myself missing her at the most random moments, like when I drank my morning coffee and thought about the ungodly amount of cream she took in hers, or when I'd seen a short blonde woman in a leather jacket in the lobby and nearly jumped out of my skin. Since then, I had taken to my bed, like a Victorian woman who had been prescribed a steady diet of gourmet chocolate to restore her constitution. I hadn't even made it to any of the New York Fashion Week shows, which I ordinarily loved. Not even the not-affiliated-with-NYFW Rex London show at Lacy's I'd been so looking forward to. Instead, I'd been holed up in here like some lovelorn shut-in with impeccable taste in both confectionery and luxury hotels.

This was not how Pepper Smith operated. I needed to get it together.

Maybe after one more truffle.

And perhaps a nap.

My phone vibrated from somewhere in the sheets. Ugh. It was probably that ghastly YouTuber again. I *never* should have kissed him. Honestly, I had no idea what I had been thinking. I kicked my phone farther down in the bed, muffling it with a duvet, resolving to deal with Auden Grace later. Or maybe never. He'd get the message eventually.

The last of the evening sun was spilling into my room, tinting everything pink. For the first time in far too long, I managed to haul myself out of bed. Pulling on a Five Seasons robe over my monogrammed silk pajama suit, I made my way over to the windows. From my room, I could see all of Central Park and the city spread around it.

There really was no place in the world like it.

New York as land of opportunity was a bit of a cliché. It made me think of some grubby Victorian urchin in a newsboy cap, pulling himself up by his bootstraps to find fame and fortune. The reality, of course, was that the story wasn't quite so simple. New York boasted the greatest income disparity in the nation, and it was quite a bit easier to pull yourself up by the bootstraps if they happened to be Hermès.

This, however, was true: New York was the ultimate place to reinvent yourself. In a city of eight million people, there were countless lives to slip in and out of, always a chance to become someone new.

How lucky for me, however, that I was born Pepper Smith.

Of course, who Pepper Smith was, exactly, could always change. A new haircut, a new address, a new business venture . . . all these changes, no matter how seemingly small, cobbled together, could result in a brand-new identity.

Most people feared starting over. Me? I relished it. There was nothing quite like the promise of possibility.

Perhaps a change was exactly what I needed after Jules. It was for the best, really, that I hadn't let her get too close. It was better not to let *anyone* get too close. After all, it was harder to change when too many people were tied to an extant version of you.

Maybe it was time to become someone new.

CHAPTER FORTY
Josie

"THAT'S IT. PAULY, I CAN'T take this anymore. Get off the highway. Now."

The tires screeched slightly as Pauly turned on the blinker and crossed two lanes of traffic to make it to the exit, the cars behind us honking their displeasure. Pauly and I exchanged a glance in the rearview mirror. Dad had never made a request like this before.

"I cannot drink one more cup of this Comfort Motel coffee!" Dad roared. "I have hit my limit! The limit is here, Pauly!" Dad indicated the limit, which was apparently about level with the brim of his fedora. "The limit is here, and I have hit it!"

"Understood, boss."

The man had lost his mind. I didn't think cheap motel coffee would be what pushed him over the edge, but here we were.

"There's a place called Rise and Grind just a couple minutes away." Figured I'd better use my phone to find Dad some real coffee, STAT. "They've got five stars on Yelp."

"Let's hope their beans are better than their puns," Dad grumbled.

Rise and Grind turned out to be in a little white wooden building not far off the highway. It had a drive-through, but Pauly parked in one of the spots right in front. Dad was out of the van before it had even come to a complete stop.

"Maybe I should invest in a portable fancy coffee machine," Pauly mused, the two of us alone in the van.

"For your sanity, that might be a good call. You want anything?"

"Nah, Josie, I'm good." He waved me away. "Try to hurry your dad along a little if you can. I want plenty of time to check out Asheville before we have to head to the venue. Did you know they call it 'Bee City USA'?"

"I did not." Wow. We were headed to Pauly's personal Disneyland. "But no problem. I'll hurry Dad along. He loves being rushed. And told what to do. And—"

"Point taken." Pauly chuckled as I hopped out of the van.

"Don't worry, Pauly," I said. "We'll get you to those bees."

The man deserved at least that much. How he'd put up with my dad on the road for all these years, I'd *never* understand.

By the time I got into the shop, ordered, and collected

my iced coffee, Dad was sitting at a round table in the window, sipping elegantly from a large, cream-colored ceramic mug.

"Got this one for here, huh?" I slid into the wooden chair across from him. "I'm not sure how well that jives with Pauly's get-to-Asheville-to-see-some-bees schedule."

"I'll take most of it to go. I just needed a couple sips from something that didn't taste like cardboard. Sometimes, it's the little things you miss the most when you're on the road."

"Mmm."

We both looked out the window then, watching the cars travel back onto the highway, where we'd be heading soon.

"But as I'm sure you've started to learn, Josie." Dad set his cup back down in the saucer. The pretty design on top of the latte was still mostly intact. "It isn't just the little things you give up when you go on the road. It's hard to unpack every night, never feeling quite at home. It's hard to keep your energy up for the same show night after night, especially when you're tired after driving all day. It's also hard"—he paused—"to form any kind of relationship, romantic or otherwise."

I looked up quickly. He was very deliberately avoiding eye contact.

"Dad. I don't know what you think is happening, but if you're referring to what I think you're referring to, I promise, there is nothing going on between me and—"

"I ran into Boone this morning as he was bidding his lady friend adieu." Dad took another sip. Wow. Okay. So we were just putting it all out there. "I know Pauly had thought there was something between the two of you . . ."

"There isn't. Wasn't. Never was." One kiss on a beach wasn't a something. "All I care about is what Boone Wyant does onstage. Whatever he does offstage makes no difference to me. And I don't need Pauly to get me a boyfriend. I'm not looking for that right now."

"Good. I just wanted to make sure you hadn't been . . . hurt."

I think this was Dad's way of showing he cared. He was kind of dancing around it awkwardly, but for him, I knew this meant something.

And maybe, what it really meant, was that he was trying. Trying to make our relationship something more than "pull up on the tempo here" and "watch your tone there."

"You have a real voice, Josie. Potentially a once-in-a-generation voice." I stared at him, openmouthed. Dad had never heaped this kind of praise on me before. "I think, with dedication, you have the potential to far surpass your old man. In terms of talent, success, everything. Everything you've always wanted can be yours, Josie. But only if—and this is a big if—you *focus*."

"I *am* focused, Dad." It was wonderful to hear him say these things, but also so frustrating. What had I ever done to make him think I lacked the focus necessary to become a star? This had always been his thing, and I've never understood it. "I know you didn't really get the Pussycats, but I always gave them my all. Just like I give everything my all when it comes to my music. Have I been anything less than professional on the tour so far?"

"You've been extremely professional."

"Thank you." At least he could acknowledge it. "And if you're still harping on about Boone, I told him, *very* clearly, that we were never going to happen. And also, clearly, from last night, he got the message."

"Understood." Dad held up his hands. "I just don't want him to distract you. I'm happy to ask him to leave the tour."

"You don't have to do that. It's fine." Asking Boone to leave the tour felt more embarrassing, like admitting I'd been hurt by him. And I hadn't been. I could keep it completely professional. He would just be another opener, nothing more. "I'm not distracted, not by Boone or by any other guy. Or anything else, for that matter."

"I'm glad to hear that." Dad sighed. "Listen, Josie. I know I'm hard on you, but I'm hard on you because you're good. And I want you to be *great*. And I think you can be."

"I appreciate that, Dad. But I also need you to start seeing me as someone who believes in her own greatness and wants it even more than you do. I'm going to be a star, Dad. I know it. And I'm not going to let anything—or anyone—stop me."

"Well, good, then. I'm glad to hear it." Dad smiled—really, genuinely smiled—and I remembered how it felt to dance around the room as a little girl while he played the piano, with complete and utter abandon, just happy to be making music with my dad.

But I was starting to wonder if it might be time for me to make music on my own.

"You know, Dad," I started, unsure how to say this, exactly, "I'm beyond grateful for this opportunity. And I've learned so much from touring with you. But—"

"You're thinking about heading out on your own," Dad finished for me. "Don't look so shocked, Josie." He chuckled. "I saw the look on your face when you sang at Tiny's. You're an artist who needs creative control. No surprise—you are *my* daughter, after all."

I had been expecting dire predictions that I'd fail. That I wasn't ready to be on my own. That leaving the tour would be a career-ending mistake.

This level of support was the *last* thing I expected.

But it felt *good*.

"I mean, you know, don't leave me on the side of the road or anything," I joked. "I'm not ready to go quite yet . . ."

"You've got a spot behind the microphone on the Myles McCoy tour for as long as you want it," Dad said sincerely. "And whenever you're ready to head out on your own, I'll be sitting front-row center on your first night."

"Thanks, Dad." I reached out and took his hand. "That means a lot."

After holding my hand for about two seconds, Dad stood up. "Well. Shall we?" For us, this had been a lot of father-daughter feelings time. "Pauly's probably lamenting the state of our schedule out there."

One to-go cup later, we were settled into our customary positions in the van and back on the highway. As we drove toward Asheville, I was excited to see what our next stop held in store. And from there, we'd head on to Pigeon Forge, Knoxville, and then, finally, Nashville. Music City.

Somehow, I doubted Boone's job offer was still on the table. But I didn't need it. And I sure wasn't going to let *him* stop me from seeing what opportunities there might be for me in Nashville. He didn't own that city. Who knows, maybe it *would* be a good place to get started. It was certainly worth checking out.

But even with all these new destinations before me, and Nashville coming closer and closer, I couldn't get New York out of my head. It seemed like the kind of place where I could become a star. Find myself. Find my voice.

It seemed like the kind of place that could be home.

EPILOGUE
Katy

"WHAT'S IN HERE?" KO PRETENDED to stagger under the weight of the cardboard box in his arms. "Dumbbells?"

"Shoes! They're just shoes!" I protested.

"That's precious cargo, KO!" Jorge scolded him jokingly. "You better get Miss Keene's fancy footwear all the way uptown without a scratch."

"I'll take good care of them." Carefully, KO navigated the towers of boxes, heading to the door. "I promise."

I knew he would, too. I could trust KO with anything important—even my shoe collection.

I put the last piece of tape on a cardboard box Jorge had helpfully marked "Eleganza Extravaganza." In seemingly no time at all, KO, Jorge, and I had packed up my childhood apartment. My entire life was tucked neatly into boxes, ready to be ferried up to Washington Heights in a truck KO had borrowed from a buddy.

I couldn't believe I was really leaving Delancey Street. Good-bye to the grooves in the floor where Mom's sewing table had scraped it. Good-bye to the red sauce stain on the ceiling from a make-your-own-pizza-night disaster. Good-bye to the millions of memories of Mom, sewing and singing and laughing and giving the best hugs.

"She'd want you to move on, Katy," Jorge said softly, putting his arm around me. "It's time."

"I know." I snuggled into him, looking out the window, past the fire escape to the buildings beyond. "And no matter where I go, I know she's always with me."

"Of course she is. And now I'll get to have you with me, too. I'm so glad an apartment opened up in my parents' building. I get a little bit of breathing space from the fam, you get the world's best roommate . . ."

"I know it." Leaving home was a lot less scary knowing that I'd have Jorge with me.

"Even with my parents giving us a break on the rent, we'll probably have to get a third roommate," Jorge mused.

"Don't worry. I bet we can find someone amazing."

"Well, that's one box on the truck." KO reappeared in the doorway. "Only about . . . a million more to go. Are the two of you planning on moving any of them?"

Before Jorge and I could answer, my phone rang. Glancing at the screen, I saw a New York area code.

"Who's calling you?" Jorge said. "Don't they know how to text like a civilized person?"

"I don't recognize the number." I frowned as the phone continued ringing. Who could it be?

"Maybe it's Lacy's?" KO suggested. "Didn't you leave them your contact information after the fashion show?

"Girl." Jorge's eyes went wide. "Get that employee discount!"

Maybe it *was* Lacy's! This could be it—a chance to work at my favorite place in the world.

Taking a deep breath, I answered the phone, hoping whoever was calling couldn't hear how loudly my heart was beating.

"Hello?"

"Katy Keene?" The voice on the other end of the line was cool and crisp, like a fresh bolt of linen, but with steel underneath the cultured tones. "This is Gloria Grandbilt. I'm calling from the personal shopping department at Lacy's."

"I know who you are," I blurted out. Gloria Grandbilt?! *The* Gloria Grandbilt was calling *me*?! "I mean, um, yes, hello. This is Katy Keene."

"Well. Glad we've established that. I may have a position available in my department. Are you available to come in for a preliminary interview?"

"Yes. Yes I am."

I flashed KO and Jorge a thumbs-up. Jorge screamed silently with glee while KO grinned, the corners of his eyes crinkling in that way I loved so much.

"Excellent. I'll have my assistant send over some potential times. We look forward to seeing you at Lacy's, Miss Keene."

"Thank you. Thank you so much."

They looked forward to seeing me at Lacy's!

I couldn't wait.

ABOUT THE AUTHOR

STEPHANIE KATE STROHM is the author of *That's Not What I Heard*; *It's Not Me, It's You*; *The Date to Save*; *Love à la Mode*; *Prince in Disguise*; and *The Taming of the Drew*. She graduated from Middlebury College with a dual degree in theater and history, and has performed in twenty-five states. She currently lives in Chicago with her husband, her son, and a dog named Lorelei Lee.